Hetty Happens!

Hetty Happens!

by

Martha Sears West

CLEAN KIND WORLD
Los Angeles

Clean Kind World
Los Angeles

Text and Illustration Copyright © 2023, 2020 Martha Sears West.
Distributed by Ingram Book Company

Hetty Happens!
Second in Series

Young Adult/Bildungsroman: This novel is a work of fiction. Names, characters,
places, and incidents are either products of the author's imagination or are used
fictitiously. All characters are fictional, and any similarity to people living or dead,
events, or locales is purely coincidental.

Publishers Cataloging-in-Publication Data
West, Martha Sears, 1938-
Hetty happens / by Martha Sears West. -Los Angeles : Clean Kind World, [2015]
pages ; cm.
ISBN: 978-1-7329799-7-0 (print) ; 978-0-9908693-3-7 (audio)
978-0-9908693-8-2 (eBook)
1. Teenagers--History--20th century--Fiction. 2. Families--History--20th century--Fiction.
3. Promises--Fiction. 4. Love stories, American. 5. Humorous stories, American. 6. Domestic
fiction. 7. Bildungsromans. I. Title.
PS3623.E449 H482 2015
813/.6--dc23 1506

The story begins in 1955, two years after the conclusion of *Hetty*.

CleanKindWorldBooks.com   ParkPlacePress.com
Toll Free 800·616·8081 · Shipping 435·764-4545 ·
Fax 323·953·9850 2016 Cummings · Los Angeles CA 90027
ymaddox@CleanKindWorldBooks.com

Martha Sears West titles are available online and in fine bookstores:
· *Jake, Dad and the Worm* · *Longer Than Forevermore* ·
· *Rhymes and Doodles from a Wind-up Toy* · *Jacques and the Forbidden Christmas*

· *Hetty, Hetty Happens, Hetty or Not, Honeymoon Summer, Hetty on Hold*
It's Me, Pippa, Love Me On Purpose, Deliriously Yours
are available in print, audio, and eBook.

10 9 8 7 6
Printed in the United States of America

For my parents,
Gordon and Elizabeth Sears,
who provided a home of exceptional
love and harmony.

With gratitude to my husband,
Steve West,
and for his fifty-four years of support
and encouragement.

Thanks to
my editor and daughter,
Page Elizabeth West Mallett,
without whose wise advice and insight
I would never have attempted this book
in the first place.

CONTENTS

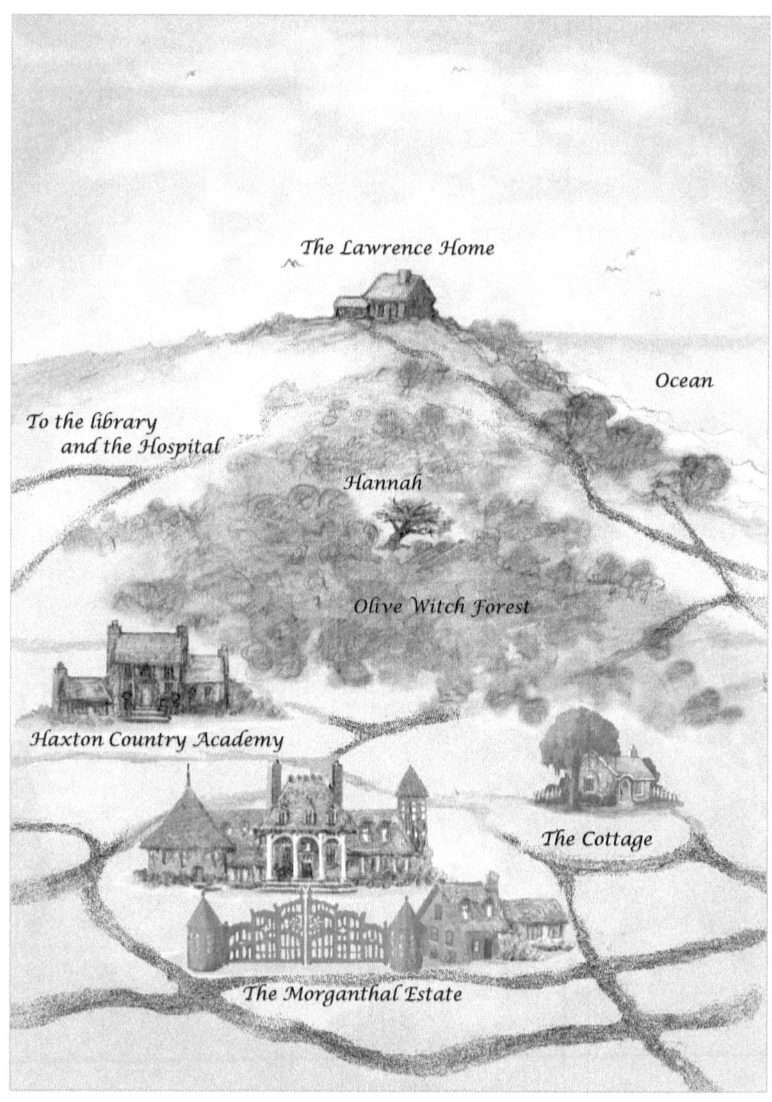

The Lawrence Home
Ocean
To the library
and the Hospital
Hannah
Olive Witch Forest
Haxton Country Academy
The Cottage
The Morganthal Estate

ILLUSTRATIONS

CHARACTERS

Hetty Lawrence *(Henrietta Annette), age 17**

Melinda Morganthal, *Hetty's classmate*

Morgan Morganthal, *Melinda's brother*

Katrinka Wallace, *Morgan's fiancée*

Leaf Locke *(Father), Hetty's natural father*

Marian Reed, *librarian and friend*

Phil Wallace, *Katrinka's father, former circus clown*

Maximilian Morganthal *(Max), father of Morgan and Melinda*

Dan and Dora Lawrence *(Papa and Mother), Hetty's adoptive parents*

Freydis Fairburn, *Leaf's sister, Hetty's aunt, school headmistress*

**This account begins in 1955, two years after the conclusion of* Hetty*.*

CHAPTER ONE

How Humiliating

Hetty arrived at school early and took her seat next to Melinda Morganthal, her best friend in all the eleventh grade.

Melinda linked arms with her. "I guess my brother's going to marry Katrinka Wallace. My parents are counting on it, you know. They're giving a sort of pre-engagement party tonight."

Hetty had expected Morgan to make the commitment sometime, but she felt a little sick now that it was real.

Melinda seemed unaware of Hetty's distress. "The servants are taking off," she said, "so my mom wonders if you could help me serve the food."

"Oh, I . . . but . . . you're sure she wants *me*?"

"She told me to ask a friend, and that's what I'm doing."

"Yes, of course I will. You know I would do anything I can for Morgan . . . for you . . . to make his plans work out perfectly. In fact, I'll even make it kind of like my mission. I promise. Morgan deserves to be happy more than anyone I know in the whole world."

That evening, after the party guests arrived, Melinda was in the dining room. Hetty found herself alone in the kitchen. She was folding tea napkins behind the pantry door when two girls entered the kitchen to talk privately. While hidden from view, Hetty overheard their hushed but animated whispers.

"You've done it again, Katrinka. You always get the cute boys. And Morgan's absolutely gorgeous!"

"He's more than just a handsome face with lots of money," said Katrinka. Her voice sounded dreamy.

"I'll say," said the other girl. "He's a real catch. Everybody knows that. And he won't stand a chance now you've set your hook for him."

"He is three years younger than I am," said Katrinka, "but I know a good man when I see one."

"Look at this place," said the other. "Even the servants' quarters are fabulous. I bet you'll be married by next spring."

Katrinka crooned her response. "I know what I want, and I've always wanted Morgan."

"Uncle Phil will use his influence, Trink. You can count on that."

"I'm not sure, Libby," whispered Katrinka. "I don't think Daddy would try that with Morgan."

"Can I be a bridesmaid?" asked Libby. "It'll be the most spectacular social event ever!"

"Shh . . . Of course. You're my only cousin."

As the two girls continued to defile the kitchen with their muffled conversation, Hetty felt nauseous. She thought,

How could they talk about him that way! "Cute" is what you call puppies. There has to be a better word to tell how his voice is so gentle and how he listens to everything you say. Morgan treats you like you're important even if you're not. A word like cute doesn't begin to explain all that.

When you're not feeling sure of yourself, Morgan can just look at you and it gives you the courage to stand a little taller.

His eyes are a really deep blue and have little flecks of brown in them.

I bet Katrinka hasn't noticed how they crinkle at the corners when he smiles.

Hetty felt a case of the hiccups coming on. Hoping to remain silent, she took a big breath, held her nose, then leaned further out of sight into the shadows of the pantry. Just as she thought her presence might go undetected, Melinda burst into the kitchen calling her name. Upon seeing Hetty's bright tangle of hair peeking out from behind the pantry door, she cried, "Oh, there you are!"

Hetty startled even herself with a loud hiccup that echoed off the walls of the kitchen and probably amused a few guests in the dining hall. Now Hetty had little choice but to come out of hiding.

As Katrinka realized she and her cousin had been overheard, a moment of silent awkwardness followed. She teetered and sputtered briefly, glaring at Hetty through the red heat of embarrassment.

Katrinka clutched Libby's hand with her primrose pink nails until regaining her composure.

Hetty decided not to tell Melinda what she had overheard. If Katrinka should capture Morgan like a fish, maybe it was because he wanted her to.

She thought of the large graceful manta rays she had once seen rising from the swells of the ocean. They came between her and Papa Dan when they were swimming. Their giant forms rose through the foam, flying high above the waves, then slapped the ocean surface before sailing one last time against the brilliant blue of the sky. The beauty of the gleaming white and black beasts left them speechless with the wonder of it.

Years later Hetty saw a large and imposing black and white manta ray mounted in a hotel lobby. She decided not to tell Dan about it. The magic of the ray's freedom and its graceful dance with the waves was over. It was just as black and white as it had been in life, but was now reduced to someone's trophy to gather dust and to be bragged over.

Oh, Morgan! Please don't let yourself be a fish hanging on the wall! I guess it's none of my business though, is it?

Though the kitchen might provide a refuge from embarrassment, Hetty couldn't stay in the pantry forever. Melinda had arranged some little lobster puffs on a lace doily, and it was her turn to pass them to the guests on a silver tray.

Hetty regretted wearing her papa's old Forest Service boots. Why had she forgotten her best shoes? She felt tall and clumsy. Maybe Morgan would see her that way too.

At least she had on her dress with the yellow sash. It looked a bit out of date though, and it didn't fit very well anymore.

In the dining hall, Hetty tried not to look straight at Katrinka, but she had never seen such a perfect-looking person and had to try consciously not to stare.

Her toenails were the same pink as her lips and they peeked flirtatiously from the front of her dainty silver shoes. Katrinka clung to Morgan's arm with a graceful ownership.

As Hetty considered this, she felt numb, and her hands turned all weak and rubbery. Without warning, the lobster puffs slipped off the platter and caused Katrinka to spill her purple drink down the front of her satin jacket. Her eyes squinted like she was trying not to squeal, but something still squeaked out between her teeth.

"Don't worry about my favorite dress, honey," she said. "I'm only sorry that you've embarrassed yourself."

Then Hetty got down on her hands and knees to pick up the lobster puffs. She didn't mean to cry, but she couldn't help it. She tried to tell Morgan she was sorry, but nothing came out. A tear dripped off the end of her nose right where she was starting to get a pimple.

She needed to reach for the handkerchief in her pocket. But Morgan took both her hands to help her stand up, and she didn't want him to let go.

"You," he whispered, "are the guest I'm happiest to see. Please allow me." He cleaned up the lobster puffs himself.

Katrinka said, "That's so sweet!"

She had absolutely perfect, pearly-white teeth and gave Morgan a smile that would melt anyone. Hetty thought her smile could catch a fish better than any hook she ever saw.

Morgan didn't see it. He was busy making sure Hetty wasn't tangled in her bootlaces.

As soon as he remembered to look at Katrinka, he introduced them. Katrinka acted like she'd never seen Hetty before.

She said, "Oh, you must be a friend of Morgan's little sister. I would be happy to show you how to fix your hair sometime, honey. It's always so satisfying to conquer something that looks as unmanageable as yours."

Hetty thought it best to tell her that would be fine, if Melinda could watch.

Katrinka gave Hetty an elegant smile. Was it so Morgan would admire her generous condescension? Hetty knew she mustn't think so unkindly of her.

That night, Hetty had trouble sleeping.

The next morning, she rose at dawn. The magnificent oak tree she called Hannah often gave her comfort, so Hetty pulled on her boots and ran into the forest. Climbing the tangled vines to Hannah's broadest branch, Hetty hoped to think more clearly there. Leaning back against the massive trunk, she closed her eyes and reviewed her painful experience.

Oh, Hannah . . . I'm absolutely mortified just thinking about last night! I hope I'll never be so embarrassed again the rest of my life.

I positively ruined Morgan's pre-engagement party. I have to make up for what I did. I promised Melinda I'd help make his plans work out. I believe in keeping promises.

But why did I ever promise to make it my mission?

And why was I so clumsy! I guess the doily was slippery. Melinda thinks the servants know some little trick to keep food from going kerplop down the neck of the Duke of Windsor, or whoever they serve. But they never told us what their tricks were.

I didn't want to look Katrinka in the eye. But when I did, I realized she was possibly the most gorgeous, magazine cover, Miss America type person I would ever see in my entire life.

She had a movie star kind of mouth. You know, the way they paint their lips like crayons going outside the lines of the coloring book but they look really gorgeous anyway. Besides that, my big toe would have filled her whole shoe, her feet were so tiny. Her high heels were absolutely skyscraper tall. Maybe she had to hang onto Morgan to keep from toppling over.

Her waist was so small that I thought of Scarlett O'Hara in Gone with the Wind. *After I read it, I asked Mother if ladies*

I've made a foolish promise.

still wore tight corsets like Scarlett did, and she said to this day you can still buy waist cinchers if you don't mind carrying smelling salts around with you just in case you pass out from not being able to breathe.

I bet Katrinka was wearing one, but she didn't faint. Probably because she had plenty of space for lungs.

Her hair had a kind of pouf on top that must have taken hours with some famous hair architect named Antoine who probably told her to sleep nose-down on her pillow for the next five days to preserve his masterpiece.

I ought to think of it as thoughtful of Katrinka to fix my hair.

Actually, I don't want to sleep standing up—or with my nose down in my pillow all week. But I thought it was best to tell her to go ahead and do it.

I've made a foolish promise. The trouble is people judge your character by how well you keep your word.

The sun was now rising above the horizon. Little blue patches of ocean were barely visible through the trees. Had she really been sitting in Hannah that long? Hetty gazed out over Olive Witch Forest and wondered at the shimmering beams of light sifting through the leaves. Hannah's branches were warm and comforting. She had every reason to be happy.

Oh, Hannah! I don't know what's the matter with me, I feel so restless. If only I could be like you, happy about the way things are, or at least resigned.

Marian Reed read me something. Willa Cather likes trees because they seem more resigned to the way they have to live than other things do. She's right about that, don't you think, Hannah?

I should be absolutely and positively content. After all, Dan and Dora are the most perfect parents ever. No matter what I call them, they'll always be my mother and papa.

It's really easy for me to be with Leaf, too. He says every day is Father's Day since he found me, and I love calling him Father.

If Dan and Leaf hadn't become friends fighting forest fires together, he might have given me to someone else. I could have been raised by an anchovy processor, or someone who breeds horseflies for export, or something awful like that.

Leaf worried about me every day for seventeen whole years — ever since I was born and my mother died. He didn't know I had a heart operation and got better.

Sometimes I stay in the cottage with him and Aunt Freydis after music night. Those recitals are really fun, even if they are mostly for family.

Dan always claps his hands till they're red and Dora taps her toes—sort of in time with the music. She sings a little off key, but nobody minds, because it's so fun to be together.

Leaf makes his violin absolutely sing. While he was growing up, no matter what instrument he chose to play, Aunt Freydis loved to accompany him on the piano. Even when he went through what he calls his "kazoo stage."

I like inviting friends to have blackberry cobbler for music night. Dora always gets to the cottage early and helps Aunt Freydis bake things that make the whole cottage smell heavenly. I'm absolutely certain heaven smells exactly like blackberry cobbler with cream and freshly grated nutmeg.

When Melinda brings her brother Morgan with her, I sing my absolute best.

Marian Reed comes when she can leave an assistant in charge of the library. Her eyes get all dreamy while she's watching Father play the violin.

Marian doesn't seem ten years older than me. Probably because she's such a good friend.

It's going to be impossible to take piano, violin, and voice lessons when I go away to college, so I'd better enjoy all three while I can.

Mother will have some good ideas for Morgan's party, and we'd better figure out the refreshments together.

Leaf and Aunt Freydis can advise me on the best music. We'll have to start rehearsing together. And we'll dedicate the recital just specially to Morgan and Katrinka.

Maybe Melinda will give me some ideas about decorating with a backdrop behind the piano.

We haven't made any specific plans like tying them together with garlands of flowers or sprinkling them with a love potion, mostly because it's nonsense. People used to put bats' blood in their potions, and that's a cruel way to repay bats for all they do for us, getting rid of mosquitoes.

We'll serenade Morgan and Katrinka with music that makes them look deep into each other's eyes and inspires them to speak rapturously of one another's various facial features.

That way, long after their fiftieth wedding anniversary, when Katrinka's wearing bifocals and has gotten all droopy, which Morgan never will, she can remember that he said her eyes were like limpid pools and made his heart race like the engine of a red Corvette, all because the music was so heavenly.

In Japan, if you want to tell your ladylove that her eyes are beautiful, you say they look like grapes. I'm serious! I guess the word for grapes doesn't sound as blunt in their language.

Limpid pools probably translates into some gross-sounding Japanese word, so people there would hear us say "limpid pools" and laugh so hard that their miso soup comes out their nostrils like what happened to me once when I was laughing and drinking grape juice.

I'm glad I have school tomorrow, so I'll have something besides last night to think about.

My pimple will probably look like Mount Vesuvius by then.

The Missing Dead Language Book

A week later, it was a sweet-smelling afternoon. School was out for the day, which was the custom before exam week in May. Hetty's plans for the music party were well under way.

She ran to Hannah and climbed to the broadest horizontal bough. Sitting high under the canopy of leaves, she gazed out over Olive Witch Forest at the soft puffy clouds playing over the ocean. They kept their distance to avoid casting shadows upon the scene.

Hetty had been eager to look through her brand-new Latin book—the one they would use next year. But she had been disappointed not to find it with her other schoolbooks when she got home from school.

Spreading the skirt of her school uniform over the warm bark, Hetty thought of it with disappointment.

If it's anything like the book we used this year, it's going to be positively delicious. In fact, that's exactly what I said to Melinda. I made sure nobody else could hear what I said.

Melinda specializes in eye rolling, so she made a wonderful cross-eyed face that absolutely could not be mistaken to mean, "Oh, yes, I agree. In fact, this Christmas I'm planning to give a Latin III textbook to everybody I know. We can all recite the

Gallic Wars together instead of singing carols and hanging our stockings by the chimney with care."

Hetty smiled to think of Melinda. She was so creative with her face. Hetty Annette Lawrence and Melinda Morganthal would probably always be seated next to each other, as long as the Haxton Country Academy for girls arranged the students alphabetically. That was fine with both of them.

Their senior year at the school promised to be another good one. Hetty had started there in the sixth grade. At first, she had known Mrs. Fairburn only as the headmistress of Haxton. Hetty's life changed dramatically when she discovered her beloved headmistress was her "Aunt Freydis," as well. Mrs. Fairburn lived near the school in a cottage she shared with her brother, Leaf Locke.

In time, Hetty made the most wonderful discovery of all: Leaf was her father.

For Leaf Locke, Hetty's birth had been shrouded in deep sorrow. Not only did his beloved wife Anne die in childbirth, but their baby was born with a defective heart. Anxious to do what was best for the little girl, he felt unprepared and inadequate to care for such a frail child himself. At the same time, his close friends, Dan Lawrence and his wife Dora, were unable to have children.

Everyone involved felt is was wise for Dan and Dora to adopt the baby, so Leaf's sister Freydis arranged for her speedy adoption.

Leaf wanted his daughter and the Lawrences to grow close and undisturbed as a family. To give them every possible advantage, he made the painful decision to step out of their lives.

For many years, he had been careful to remain undiscovered; however, after his chance discovery of Hetty, Leaf and Freydis watched over her quietly and undetected for three years. They loved the child and spoke of her as Annette, or little Anne.

Flying

These were the things on Hetty's mind when she heard the soft rustle of dry leaves. She looked down from her perch in the giant tree, into the clearing beneath her. Morgan Morganthal was there.

With his dark thatch of hair and thick eyebrows, Morgan's appearance reflected the heaviness of his home responsibilities. He devoted much of his energy to his sister Melinda's happiness, for there was little contact between the Morganthal parents and their two children. Morgan and Melinda were seen mainly as an inconvenience, as they interfered with an active social life. The Morganthal home was very different from Hetty's, which was brimming with love.

Morgan cleared his throat, almost with reverence, as if to acknowledge this was a private place in which he ought not to speak uninvited.

Hetty's smile of surprise and pleasure provided the consent he thought necessary, so he spoke.

"I hope you don't mind. I've come with your Latin book," he said, holding it up for her to see. "Melinda must have gathered it up with her own things."

Hetty imagined she could see his words floating up in the golden flecks of sunlight, parting the branches. The leaves seemed to flutter their quiet approval of his presence. She thought, *Morgan isn't saying how he knew where to find me.*

Father Leaf must have told him where I'd be, but Morgan didn't say so. That means he was willing to take the blame onto himself, in case I didn't want him to come here.

Hetty looked down toward the tangled vines emerging from the forest floor. She almost willed them to put forth a welcoming appearance. Hannah seemed to understand Hetty's trust, and a ray of dappled sunlight fell across the vines, indicating the way to Hetty's private world.

Morgan reached her quickly with the book.

Looking at the wide view before him, Morgan appeared suddenly thoughtful. It seemed to Hetty as if the whispered words of some dream were trying to come from his lips. For a time, he quietly watched the distant clouds billow above the blue patches of the sea.

If Morgan hoped for an excuse to delay his departure, he found it when Hetty eventually interrupted the stillness.

"This is Hannah," she said. Then she heard herself add, "She's a tree." Hetty flushed. She thought how foolish these obvious words must sound.

I don't blame old-fashioned people for saying things like "Twas the dawn of the day," or "Ah, the dew from heav'n distilleth, forsooth." At least it shows an effort to be charming or something. But what possible excuse could there be for my saying, "She's a tree!"

That sounded so idiotic! If I were Melinda, I would for sure be rolling my eyes or going cross-eyed.

A smile crinkled the corners of Morgan's eyes. His face was so friendly that she forgot to feel embarrassed about what had escaped her mouth. She thought,

I hope he will sit here forever and ever, so the smell of him will cling to Hannah and his voice will blend with the wind, and we'll both fly up through the leaves and he'll pull me up beyond the clouds. Like eagles high above the sun, lifting each other. Higher and higher toward the light . . . brighter and brighter, until the perfect day . . . Don't let go, Morgan . . .

Oh, don't let go!

Hetty looked down at her hand and realized it was gripping the Latin III textbook.

"Thank you," she said. "I should have kept better track of it myself."

Different Worlds

Morgan scarcely heard her words. The branches surrounding them swayed in the soft breeze. The scent of honeysuckle reached his nostrils . . . or was it Hetty's breath . . . Morgan marveled at her curls as they lifted, light as sea foam. Or was it feathers . . .

His thoughts went back to when he was seven years old and he was jumping on a featherbed. His grandmother said, *Morgan, stop that right now, or it's going to burst!* She asked his father, *Can't you control him?* then she added, *He's your son!*

Morgan was about to stop jumping, when he heard his father grumble, "*Unfortunately,*" and the two grownups stormed out of the room.

Morgan's jumping then became frenzied and confused. His little fists flailed the air and battered the soft bedding. Anger and tears came in waves, and his grunts became a loud and lonely wailing. Feathers were everywhere, and Morgan was in the middle of them.

After a time, he grew quiet and straightened his shoulders. Morgan thought of his baby sister Melinda. They had each other, and Melinda was someone who loved him.

He went into the room where the plump child was sleeping, and gathered her up. Together they blew the downy fluff lightly into the air like bath bubbles. It made her laugh from her belly as only a three-year-old can do. She gave him a big soggy kiss he didn't bother to wipe off. Morgan decided he would always take care of Melinda.

The word *unfortunately* still hovered over him, but it wasn't going to hurt any more.

The leaves surrounding Hetty shimmered in the soft breeze. Morgan watched a blush of pink spreading across her cheeks. It swirled in his head together with flecks of dancing sunlight. Weightless as swan's down, the pale wisps of her hair captured the glow to form a silken halo. He wanted to spread his wings and fly above the world.

I want to reach for the light I see around her. If she could fly with me through the clouds . . . beyond the sky, and higher. Where everything is clean and bright . . . bright and beautiful . . . and never let go.

Hold my hand, Hetty! Hold tight . . . hold tight!

Morgan realized he was gripping a branch. He released his hold, blinked, and quickly looked away from Hetty.

He resolved to stop noticing her altogether.

Morgan tried to revise his thinking, and gazed at the distant clouds. He must no longer imagine soaring above the clouds with outstretched wings. Not with Hetty. It was time for real life.

He remembered . . . *Katrinka's waiting for me back at the gatehouse. She's here in town to see me, so it won't do for me to neglect her. Katrinka wasn't my idea, but I need to give her a chance.*

Getting engaged to her might be the one way I could hope to get my father's approval.

"I guess you and my sister will be sitting together again this year," he said to Hetty. Morgan thought how pleasant it must be to sit next to Hetty.

If Hetty weren't going to a girls' school, the boy behind her would probably dip her braids in his inkwell to get her attention, or bring her candy with corny notes, like, "Here's some candy for someone dandy." I know I would if I were her age.

Maybe she would let me carry her books while I recite the names of all the elements, maybe the planets, and the Gettysburg Address. I could conjugate a few Latin verbs. I think that kind of thing would impress her.

Then we could sit at the soda fountain of Whittlesey's Drug store and share a sarsaparilla float. She'd appreciate the soda jerk being a good friend of mine, and the way he would give us an extra scoop of ice cream.

Then Hetty would ask me all about my Forest Service job last summer. She already knows a lot about fighting fires from both Dan, who adopted her, and her father, Leaf.

Maybe I shouldn't tell her everything about being a smoke-jumper though, like how long we had to go without showers, and what we went through when they trained us. But I could tell her about the fire where the pilot of the Ford tri-motor dropped me on the spike of a pine tree and I swung from my parachute over the embers. She would listen with her eyes wide and ask me to tell it to her all over again.

What am I thinking? We're in two different worlds. None of this will ever happen. Instead of dreaming, I should just be content to know Melinda can sit next to her.

CHAPTER TWO

The Father-Father-Daughter Party

A few days later, Hetty smoothed her flowered tablecloth across Hannah's broadest branch and leaned back to do some thinking.

It's going to be Haxton Academy's very first Father-Daughter party, eight days from now. Melinda doesn't know what to do. She's on the committee, and she's been counting on Morgan to take her. The trouble is he said no, it wouldn't make sense. I was kind of surprised, because he goes to lots of parent-teacher meetings and things like that for Melinda.

I told her I would be happy to share one of my fathers with her, which was an outright lie. I've really been looking forward to taking both Dan and Leaf to it.

I suggested she use her most pitiful cross-eyed pouty face to let Morgan know how terribly important to her it was for him to come. She said it probably wouldn't be any fun anyway, because there are always lots of girls hanging around trying to get Morgan's attention. He's too polite to shoo them away. I know how that can be. It's sort of that way with Father Leaf, too.

One time I mentioned to Leaf how Dan and Dora said he was considered an extremely eligible gentleman. He laughed and said I must have heard wrong; the word they had meant was undoubtedly "illegible," because his handwriting is so loopy and impossible to read. Then I told him in that case, they might have said "unintelligible," 'cause having unreadable writing makes people not understandable.

Shouldn't the opposite of un-derstandable be "derstandable? That's a new word Leaf and I made up.

I'd better go up to the house before my parents get home from work. Papa might have some idea how to go about spreading fathers around.

Hetty climbed the hill to her home. A couple of years earlier, the house had been ripped up and washed out to sea when a wedge tornado destroyed the hilltop on which it stood. Dan was rebuilding it, and the pleasant scent of paint and new lumber inside was still fresh. Their home promised to look and feel very much as it did before its destruction.

Immediately after the disaster, Leaf and Aunt Freydis had opened not only their cottage to the three of them, but their lives, as well. Hetty and her parents had felt completely at home staying there in the cottage until their own place was ready. Hetty would always savor the memory of the five of them living together. During that time the respect and admiration they all felt for one another added an aura of electric excitement to whatever they did together. The affection the four adults felt for Hetty was expanded by the mutual sharing of it.

Hetty stood at the kitchen window. At any moment, Dan and Dora should be coming home from work. While watching for them, it saddened her to see the condition of the graceful elm trees that lined the driveway.

It reminded her of what she'd learned of the word *decimation*, in her Latin class. The teacher said it meant literally *removal of a tenth*. When a Roman commander chose to punish the offenses of a large unit, he would divide the soldiers into groups of ten, and execute the one unfortunate man of each group whose lot it was. The punishment of the remaining nine of them was just to receive barley rations instead of wheat, for three days.

Hetty looked at the elm trees. The tornado had mangled or completely destroyed about a tenth of the stately elms, and much of the hilltop was still bare. The word decimation remained on her mind.

Suppose you were a soldier whose unit was decimated. Maybe you'd be one of the lucky nine whose only punishment was three days of barley. Every time you thought of barley, would it forever remind you of how close you came to being executed? If so, I suppose it would make you feel ill just to think of it. I guess you wouldn't even like beef and barley soup the way Dora makes it.

If it happened to me, maybe I would always love barley, because it would remind me to be thankful for being alive. At least I hope I could make myself feel that way.

Soon after Dan and Dora arrived, the three of them sat at the kitchen table. Dora poured three tall glasses of milk to accompany the oatmeal cookies she had made. Hetty watched Dan's face and spoke to him of the school party.

"I want both you and Leaf to go with me, Papa. But maybe Melinda will think I'm selfish for not sharing," she said.

"It's important for you to take your father after he spent all those years without you," he said. "But don't expect me to give up my position as your Papa," he added with a wink, "even for one night."

Dan brushed cookie crumbs from the front of his suit. "Tell me something, Hetty. If Morgan doesn't think it would work for him to go with his sister, did he have another suggestion?"

"Not really," said Hetty. "Morgan just told Melinda she should invite their dad, but of course she won't. He'd say no, anyway."

Dan Lawrence looked directly at his daughter. Hetty knew what that look meant, and she sensed there was some responsibility that went along with her being able to read his expression.

I know just what he's thinking. He's right. It doesn't cost a thing to be optimistic, and we usually pay a higher price for expecting the worst.

Hetty looked away while she thought about it.

Isn't it up to Melinda to think of that on her own? It's not my place to tell other people what's right. It's really none of my business. Besides, Mr. Morganthal won't want to go anyway. I don't think he cares about Morgan and Melinda. He'll always be like that.

Actually, I know Papa would want me to be careful with the words "never" and "always." Even when it has to do with Mr. Morganthal.

If I tell Papa what I'm thinking, he'll ask me if I'd like to mull it over a little longer, in case there's another way to look at it.

Maybe I should.

Hetty looked across the table again. By the time she was ten she had already outstripped Dora. Now she was taller than Dan. When they needed things from the upper cupboards, she liked helping them.

She had never thought much about being tall one way or the other, but now Hetty enjoyed being with Leaf when people said things like, "Aha! So that's where you got your height!"

She looked at her papa and thought fondly of her many conversations with him.

You never tell me what to do. You always make me work it out for myself. You say if I can't find how to accomplish something, I should make it happen anyway. Then you leave me on my own to figure out how.

It's kind of like our school motto, Inveniam viam aut faciam. I shall find a way or make one. . . . Actually, Melinda sees the motto every day at school, too!

Too bad I can't just put it on flash cards and run it in front of her lots of times during class. Like the way they use subliminal messaging in the movies.

Right in the middle of a Popeye cartoon, these chipmunks tell you how delicious some brand of donuts are. They talk so fast you don't even know you heard it, but your brain gets the message. Then at intermission everyone lines up with their mouths watering, to buy jelly donuts. Even people who never liked them before and think they're too sticky to eat in the theater.

Anyway, maybe I can find some way to help Melinda think positively about asking her dad.

Rising Above Froghood

Dan seemed to read his daughter's thoughts.

"Maximilian Morganthal." He stated the name deliberately and then paused to look out the window. Producing a red handkerchief, he gave his nose an impressive honk. "Max is one of my clients. He is an honest man," said Dan, "and he's generous. It might be good for Melinda to take her brother's advice. Everyone needs to be given a chance."

Hetty had seen Mr. Morganthal only a few times. The word "chiseled" might describe his face. He had the same well-defined features and deep blue eyes as Morgan, but they were cold and steely. His chin was square, and the set of his jaw made him appear ready to grind his teeth.

Hetty continued to think.

As an attorney, Papa never says anything about what goes on between him and his clients, but maybe he knows how Morgan got the bruises we've sometimes seen, and whether they're connected with his father. Maybe Mr. Morganthal punishes Morgan for something like humming under his breath or losing the cap to the Ipana toothpaste.

One time I heard how marriages are actually destroyed sometimes by little things like that. So the way to save your marriage is to purposely throw away the lid to the toothpaste first thing when you buy it. After you do that, nobody will have to take the blame.

I suppose if a happy marriage depends on how careful you are with the new car, you'd need to scratch the paint right away and smash the left headlight before it even goes in your garage the first time.

The next morning, Melinda passed a note to Hetty. She had scrawled the question, "Which of your fathers do I get to take?"

Hetty wrote her answer on the back. "Let's talk during lunch."

Hetty often did her best thinking high among Hannah's leaves, so during study period she tried to imagine sitting on a broad branch with Melinda, swinging their feet together.

Hetty invented a possible conversation.

"This warm spot in the sun is just for you, Melinda. Lean back and make yourself comfortable."

"Oh, Hetty, you're so lucky. I wish my parents loved me. You have so many people who think you are absolutely the center of their universe. If Morgan really cared about me, maybe he would go to the father-daughter party, but he won't because he thinks I should try asking our father."

"Dear Melinda, I truly understand the depth of your sorrow. If Morgan were my brother, his company at any event

would be the greatest honor I could ever hope for. If he danced with me I would never wash my hand where he touched mine, and if he went to the refreshment table to bring me a piece of poppy seed cake, I would take it home in my purse and keep it pressed it in the encyclopedia forever, under 'M' for Morgan."

"Do you think one of your fathers would come with me?" asked Melinda.

"Well here's what I think," said Hetty. "I think your own father has a secret longing to be recognized as the most beloved father ever. He's waiting for someone to understand the desires of his heart, and notice the depth of his desire to be changed from a frog into a prince, or into a knight in shining armor who is so brilliant he can help you with any homework you could name including the names of all the countries and their capitals, no matter how often they change.

"I wonder if one reason he is a bit more of a frog than you might hope is because that's what you think he is. Maybe he will rise to the occasion if he thinks he is your prince. Papa says everyone is susceptible to improvement.

"Imagine, Melinda, if you had been older than him, and he just happened to be born as your son instead of your dad. Maybe you could have raised him to know how to be a really good father. Maybe he didn't have a chance while he was growing up."

"I know you're right, Hetty. You are wise beyond your years. And yet it does make you wonder how it happens that my brother Morgan didn't have any example to learn from, yet he's absolutely perfect anyway. He used to sing me to sleep and read me Winnie-the-Pooh and he's so strong and fun and clever and has such good manners, and he takes such care to protect me, and. . . ."

Hetty saw she ought to change the direction of her thoughts.

I guess it won't help to think about Morgan. No . . . I need more ideas about Melinda inviting her father.

Hetty looked up at Miss Altoona, who was monitoring the study hall. The floor boards beneath her squeaked with each pace, as if to warn the girls to concentrate on their studies, or else they wouldn't get admitted to Radcliffe and would lead lives of woeful ignorance, heaping disappointment and sorrow upon all those expecting them to at least win the Nobel Peace Prize, if not better.

Hetty redirected her thinking.

I'd better finish my history homework. Miss Altoona has her little notebook and red pencil with her. She can see right through our brains, and I don't want her to put a little red mark next to my name when she sees what's in mine. It's not history homework.

But I can't help thinking of something Papa told me. He says we have an obligation to lift each other and to be lifted, as members of the family of mankind.

I think that's what I'll tell Melinda at lunch. I won't have time to practice saying that in front of the mirror to make it sound impressive, so she'll probably just pull her cross-eyed face and laugh her head off.

But if Melinda wants to help her dad rise above froghood, maybe she'll listen.

Waiting

It was the night of the father-daughter party. There was a general buzzing and whispering at Haxton Academy as the students and their fathers entered the reception hall.

They wondered who could have magically transformed the space. It deserved so little notice on ordinary days, but on this night it was an enchanted world. Streamers and spangles, posters of circus animals, and brightly colored awnings greeted the guests at both ends of a red-carpeted bridge.

Mrs. Fairburn had given Melinda Morganthal the responsibility of decorating for the party. Among the decorations were many things Hetty and Morgan had helped to bring to school from Melinda's bedroom. Several silhouettes Melinda had painted were cleverly displayed and illuminated with colored lanterns.

The place looked magnificent, and Hetty knew why. Maximilian Morganthal would be coming. Melinda was hoping to begin a friendship with her father in this very room.

Hetty felt Melinda's nervous energy. She watched her tend to a few details, with one eye on the door, awaiting the arrival of her father. Melinda's face was flushed, and she turned to Hetty repeatedly to ask if her slip was showing or if there was anything amiss in her appearance. It would not have helped to tell Melinda how positively giddy she appeared, with such a radiant smile on her face.

Hetty felt the force of Melinda's many emotions: her expectant and boundless joy; the kind of indescribable happiness that comes when the race is almost won and you taste the blood of your exertion with every breath; when the running is almost over, confidence swells and you wish for everyone to share in the joy by winning with you; when it would ruin nothing to see the entire world triumphant.

Then you fling your body over the finish line, and smell the newly mown grass when you lie stretched out, panting, under a pleasant breeze.

At last the person you were running for seems to notice you, with just a sideways glance, and brings you a cool glass of water. He might even say something nice like, *I didn't know you could run like that.*

How could you ask for anything more?

Throughout the evening, Melinda sat with Hetty, Dan and Leaf. With their help, she was able to keep a smile pasted to her face, though her back was straight and stiff. The tears she had not shed must never spill over.

Hetty was attentive to Melinda in every possible way.

When Dan invited Melinda to dance, they laughed good-naturedly about how the music must be at fault for the general entanglement of their feet.

With Leaf as her partner, she swayed and swirled with the grace of a princess.

At the close of the festivities, the music stopped, and the bright lights were unplugged. Decorations were removed by the clean-up committee, as yawning girls stepped over a confusion of tape and torn paper to gather their coats.

Melinda stood alone with her back to the door. As she looked over the room that had held so much promise, she didn't notice the handsome dark-haired gentleman who entered in silence and walked toward her.

She heard only, "May I have the honor of this dance?"

Then it all seemed to play out in slow motion. Her hair

with the lace ribbons, the tiny pearl beads around her neck, and the rose satin dress with the stiff crinolines under the skirt all moved together. Melinda slowly turned to face her father, the cause of all her shattered hopes. Perhaps the pieces of herself, so nearly broken, would crumble now.

While Leaf and Dan went for the car, Hetty returned to retrieve her friend. There she saw Maximilian Morganthal trying to pin a corsage to Melinda's shoulder. He couldn't keep it from flopping over. Struggling with the pin, they laughed. Then he knelt on the floor to feel around for it until Melinda discovered it was caught in the left cuff of his pants.

The party was successful. Max Morganthal had come.

The next morning Hetty ran to Hannah where she could review the satisfaction she had felt at the father-daughter party.

If only Morgan could have been there it would have made the dance even better. Hetty relived a few other memories with Hannah.

I keep thinking about how the PTA likes us to have dances at school. It's probably so we'll get used to socializing with boys before we go off to college. That way, the first time one of them actually talks to us, we won't go into a tizzy and write home about it then start crocheting doilies and dishcloths for our hope chest or something.

Actually, what we mostly learned from the dances is that boys do an awful lot of refueling at the refreshment table. At our first dance, the boys all filled their punch cups and headed for where the girls were lined up against the other wall, but the punch never made it that far, so they'd have to keep going back for more.

Once they got their hands good and sticky with punch and cookies, they'd start kind of circling us to figure out how tall we each were. But they'd never look us right in the eye. It's like there was an unwritten rule that if they ever did look directly at us, they'd be committed to dance the next ten dances with us. Even if it was the kind of dance nobody knows how to do, like a samba, which is one of the reasons the refreshment table is so popular.

I hardly ever got to dance, which was all right with me, because it meant nobody got me all sticky with punch.

Then everything changed when Morgan started coming. The reason he got invited was because one time when he went to a PTA meeting about Melinda, somebody there knew he was a volunteer at the Edgemont Senior Community Center. They said he was good at helping people who were in wheelchairs to sort of do a waltz or a foxtrot and have fun.

The parents drafted him to be on our school dance committee to keep us all mixing better. So he went, but not like a chaperone or anything like that. Morgan says they chose him because he could make it all the way across the dance floor with a full punch cup.

The best thing was that whenever Morgan came, he made sure there weren't any girls just sitting there like wallflowers. He got some of the other boys mixing around as well.

He used a couple of different memory systems to keep people's names straight in his mind. One way was to rhyme either their first or last names with something. Like Nona Morris with chorus, and Michelle with pastel because she was wearing pastel colors. One time, a really embarrassing thing happened. After he'd been dancing with Eliza Tummock, they traded with another couple, and he introduced Eliza Tummock as Eliza Kelly. His face was absolutely beet red. It was a real struggle to keep from laughing, but we were able to keep Eliza from noticing,

As long as we'd lost our composure anyway, while we danced, Morgan and I invented some new lyrics that sounded sort of like the words in "The Tennessee Waltz."

Instead of "I remember the night and the Tennessee Waltz," the words we sang were, "I will never fly kites sipping strawberry malts." After the next dance he looked for me to see if I liked another one he made up. It went, "Whenever I fly, it's the chimpanzee's fault."

When it was a girl's choice dance, I was afraid it would seem too forward to cut in on his partner. There were too many other girls with the same idea, so I didn't get to tell him the one I'd thought of. It was, "September's the time for ten somersaults."

Melinda thinks the reason her brother dances more with me is because I'm her friend. I think it's because Morgan notices the other boys hardly ever ask me. They would look too short next to me. Boys don't usually like that, but I guess Morgan doesn't care.

M Is for Mockingbird

Morgan had been lying awake waiting for Melinda to return from the father-daughter party. He was surprised to see the sparkle in her eyes and the orchid pinned to her dress. She talked breathlessly and with such animation that Morgan didn't mind her repeating herself. He realized his sister needed to relive the magical night of dancing with their father, because such a thing might never again occur.

"Tonight only happened because you were so stubborn," she laughed. "At the time, I thought you were just being mean, refusing to come."

Morgan socked his pillow and grinned at her. Locking his hands behind his head, he lay back to watch and listen.

Melinda flopped down across the bottom of his bed, and added, "I figured it out about Hetty. You put her up to it! You got her to make that speech . . . about giving Dad a chance . . . and how he was waiting to be a wonderful father, and all that."

Morgan raised his eyebrows. *Hetty. It was Hetty,* he thought. He was determined not to talk about it, or to have Melinda read his thoughts, so he poked her in the ribs with his big toe until she squealed and went off to her own room, laughing.

He lay awake thinking. Good things don't just happen on their own; it takes someone good like Hetty to make them happen.

The next morning while Morgan was shaving, the image he faced in the mirror seemed to be his father's instead of his own. It startled him to realize how connected they were and always would be.

As he was leaving the house, he saw a book under his father's scarf and gloves. It appeared to have been left there in haste the night before. The name of the book was *Alcoholics Anonymous*.

So that's where his father had gone last night! Instead of going straight to the father-daughter party, Max Morganthal had gone to an Alcoholics Anonymous meeting. There might be more peace at home in the future. Maybe things would get better, but Morgan wasn't going to count on it.

Following a path worn by many woodland creatures, Morgan walked into the forest to find Hetty; to thank her for showing such thoughtfulness toward Melinda.

At the very time Morgan had seen some slight chance their home life might improve, it was Hetty's goodhearted influence that made all the difference.

It would be ungrateful not to acknowledge her kindness, he thought.

If I find her, I mustn't stay where I can see her for very long. I should thank her and leave quickly. I must never again imagine things that can't happen.

I mustn't get too close. She makes me think of possibilities and dreams . . . of how everything can be good, and I want to reach up . . . and keep reaching until everything I find is right and I feel strong, and the power I feel is all brightness and light, almost as though I'm flying when I'm near her. If only I could rise to where she is, I could fly with her forever.

No, maybe I'd better go back home.

I need to call Katrinka. She wants me to take her to get a manicure. I think she wants her left hand to look perfect in case I buy her a ring.

I can't imagine myself at a jewelry store listening to her ooh and ahh over diamonds.

How would she fit into my life if I stayed with the Forest Service? I wonder how she'd enjoy showing her engagement ring to the bears and mountain lions if we live in a lookout.

I could suggest she ask for a manicure on just her left hand. She could leave her other one for pretending she's a real person who actually uses her hands for ordinary worthwhile purposes;

someone who doesn't worry about chipping her nails or doesn't mind touching things that need to be washed off.

Or doing things like climbing trees.

Morgan came to the edge of the clearing. Holding aside a lacy curtain of leaves, he stepped quietly across the ferns and into the dappled sunlight before him. The magnificent Hannah rose overhead like a vaulted ceiling of a cathedral.

A sheet of loose notepaper fluttered near his feet, catching his attention. He reached down to retrieve it. There were several lines erased, and words were crossed out here and there in an apparent effort to replace good words with better ones. Morgan wondered if it might be Hetty's schoolwork, and turned it over absently.

He stared for some time at the completed verses on the other side. The heading was simply "For M," and it was followed by a poem. The lines were written in carefully formed letters. He puzzled over what the letter M might stand for.

For M

> *Come fly into my dreams again!*
> *I long for you to stay;*
> *To set your wings for heaven,*
> *And carry me away.*

> *And if you whisper, "Take my hand,"*
> *Our bright and perfect day*
> *Will linger in my dearest dreams*
> *When you have flown away.*

He read it a second and a third time, with even greater interest. It was not meant for his eyes, and he knew he should put it down. He was thinking he should quietly take his leave without seeking Hetty any further. And for fear of being discovered, Morgan avoided rustling leaves or stepping on twigs underfoot.

A noisy mockingbird began its mimicry overhead. Morgan looked up to see it performing from a broad, sun-drenched branch. Hetty had been asleep on a limb nearby. She sat up quickly and her eyes widened as she saw Morgan and the paper he clutched in his hand.

Realizing he had been discovered, it seemed only right that he should offer to deliver the scrap of paper to her. There was no question; she seemed most eager to have it back.

In no time, she was reaching for it and hoping he hadn't read her poem.

Maybe it will be something else. If I'm lucky, some careless person was running an errand for his wife, and dropped his shopping list on the way to the store. It'll just say, "Five ripe bananas; Ovaltine; two Idaho potatoes."

No, it wasn't a shopping list. It was her poem, all right. Hetty held it a very long time. It was as if she'd never seen it before. Now that she saw it through Morgan's eyes, it seemed quite embarrassing to her. The color crept up Hetty's neck and into her cheeks.

Although Morgan's original mission had been to thank her, it had completely left his head. He tried to think of something to say that might relieve the awkwardness of the moment.

*He looked away to allow Hetty
to regain her composure.*

Let's see . . . there's always the weather. "It looks like there's plenty of weather going on out here, today, ha ha!" Or maybe I could tell her the joke about the Mexican weather report: chili today, and hot tamale.

Morgan was still groping for words, when Hetty tried rather uncertainly to answer the question that loomed so insistently between them.

She spoke with a trembling voice. "Mockingbird begins with 'M,'" she said. Her hands quickly covered her face, but he could still see the pink color between her fingers.

Perhaps a serious discussion would put her at ease. It would be unkind to leave her now, at the height of her discomfort. He looked away to allow Hetty to regain her composure, and began.

"An interesting thing happened in Madrid this year. The U.S. gliding team did very poorly in the competition over there. Because of that, there should be a tremendous push to succeed in the next one."

Hetty wondered how that fact applied to Morgan, and she gave him her full attention. "It's coming up too soon for me to compete next time around," he continued, "but I have enough hours in the air to fly solo now."

There was an unmistakable expression of excitement and disbelief on her face. Her eyes were asking him to tell her everything he could possibly think of about gliders, like how it felt when the thermals lifted him above the clouds. Did the birds seem to mind sharing space in the sky, and could he see the world curve away on all sides?

"Soon," he said, "I'll qualify to take a passenger."

Morgan wondered at the unplanned words he heard

come from his own mouth. Hetty had extracted them like an eager child, and they popped out much like the clown in a Jack-in-the-box. Now they spun around in his head to complicate his life.

Winning the Horserace

Morgan tossed restlessly in his bed that night. Both he and Melinda felt most of their happy childhood experiences had been created by Katrinka's father, and they were grateful for his kindness.

Morgan thought about how Phil Wallace had taken him and sometimes his little sister Melinda for ferryboat rides along with Katrinka. And there were many long lazy drives among the hills across the river.

They often walked to the ocean's edge for a picnic. It was Morgan's job to carry the creaky picnic basket woven by Indians. After nibbling on fried chicken and poppy seed cakes, he and Katrinka would play together in the surf or bury each other in the warm sand.

Shortly after Phil's wife died, Katrinka had her ninth birthday. At first Phil had no idea what to do for a birthday party. When he finally suggested Katrinka could celebrate by inviting a friend to the movies, it was no surprise when she chose Morgan.

They saw a double feature of two horse movies, *Flicka* and *Florian,* plus a newsreel and a Popeye cartoon. After the movie, the two of them played in the park while Phil napped on a soft quilt his wife had embroidered.

Katrinka practiced her best whinny and Morgan galloped as convincingly as any six-year-old with only two legs could possibly do. He drew a starting gate in the dirt so they could pretend to be racehorses. Morgan assured her the race would be fair because they were about the same size and height.

Katrinka lost the first race by a big margin. But she said that was okay with her, because she knew about a sort of a rule. "This is how it goes," she said authoritatively. "Whoever loses has to kiss the other person."

Even at the age of six, Morgan was not inclined to lose at anything that required manly strength or speed. However, Katrinka lost every race after that with hardly any effort at all.

Morgan rather enjoyed Katrinka's affection but was glad there was nobody nearby to see how much of it she kept planting on his cheeks. He had already been teased by a few friends who could see she was sweet on him. But most embarrassing of all, she was much prettier than Shirley Temple.

When her last squeaky kiss landed smack on his lips she said, "There! Now that means we'll get married for real when we get big."

"You mean when I'm older than you?" he asked.

"No, silly! I'll always be older. But you'll be bigger than me. Not a dwarf like Daddy," said Katrinka.

"Now we have to make a promise, real solemn and everything," she added.

Morgan hopped on one foot in pursuit of a green grasshopper. "Okay," he said.

He was glad to know when he grew to be a man there would be someone he could play with. They would of course need to get a new deck of cards to play *Go Fish or Old Maid,* because they had lost a few cards from each deck.

He could belong to Katrinka in a different way than Melinda, but he would of course keep it secret. Morgan liked knowing he was special to someone.

Soon after that ninth birthday, Phil sent Katrinka away to boarding school. The next eleven years Phil longed for his daughter. Treasuring every letter she sent, he read and reread each one until they were in tatters. During that lonely time his warm relationship with Morgan was a comfort to him.

Morgan wondered if he was seeing a different Katrinka now. How much had she changed? He pulled the pillow down tightly over his face and wondered if the new Katrinka might give him that same smothered feeling. He raised the pillow to gasp in the fresh air. Morgan continued to worry.

Katrinka says she doesn't ever want me to fly because she worries about me. She seemed especially worried about my safety last time. Was it only because we'd be missing the country club dance? She thought there might be a lot of important people I ought to meet. I even told her I could do both. When I said I'd throw a tuxedo over my jumpsuit at the last minute, she didn't think it was at all funny.

Morgan decided to be fair he must keep an open mind. He would wait and see.

CHAPTER THREE

In the Circus Business

Wherever Dora Lawrence found herself, the surroundings seemed to be intended for taller people. Dan told her he was pretty sure once upon a time the architects of the world went around measuring only the tallest human beings. From that time on, all kitchen counters were designed so tall people like the Watusi tribesmen of Africa or the Royal Prussian guards could knead the dough for their Parkerhouse rolls without bending over.

Dora was quite sure her ancestors had not been among those measured. She thought of this while standing on a stool to polish the office window. The far corners were just out of reach.

She looked through the gold and black letters which spelled out *Daniel Lawrence, Attorney at Law,* across the middle of the window, and saw a gentleman with a distinct and rather aristocratic appearance. He was coming up the stairway toward the front door. The man seemed not so much regal as strikingly sure of himself, and accustomed to having his way.

Normally the front doorknob stuck. People would rattle it a few times, mumbling unpleasant words under their breath before it would cooperate and open into the waiting room. Among the foot shuffling confusion of tangled coat sleeves, lost keys, and dropped gloves, Dora had the job of soothing ruffled feathers before indicating the door into her husband's book-lined office. However, Dora knew the client about to come through the entrance would do so with grace and dignity. He would introduce himself as Maximilian Morganthal, as he had on his previous visits, then wait for her to offer him a seat.

Max nodded courteously in her direction then offered his hand to help her from the stool and safely to the floor. He exuded a formality to which Dora was not accustomed; however, it never occurred to Dora to feel uncomfortable under any circumstances. To her, all people were friends, whether they realized it yet or not.

She offered him a homemade oatmeal cookie, and she did it with a warmth that seemed to take him completely by surprise. Now disarmed, his rather cool and distant expression almost softened.

Dora pushed back some little wisps of her hair with her small hands and smiled. Looking directly into his eyes, she said, "Your son and daughter are fine people. You must be proud of them."

Maximilian was in Dan's office just over an hour. After his departure, Dan sat quietly looking out the office window and thought about all they had discussed.

Max Morganthal. . . . There's so much wealth that's come down through his wife's family. How is it he's had so little experience with business decisions before now? There are the banks, insurance companies, travel agencies, newspapers, fashion design houses, shipbuilding, and so on. The circus is the least successful of all.

Max is a complicated man. He showers Melinda and Morgan with extravagant gifts, yet he feels uncomfortable spending time with them. It makes him angry to see how Melinda turns to her brother Morgan with her problems. He envies Morgan because he does everything right.

Just when life was about to get better for them, they were so full of hope . . . now that he and his wife are attending Alcoholics Anonymous meetings . . . a completely new burden is dropped on him. He'll have full responsibility for the circus. I can't imagine how he's going to cope with it.

Even so, with Phil and Morgan's help, it could become productive and well run. I hope I can be of some assistance.

He should be asking Morgan for advice, instead of trying to get him married and out of the house.

Always

It was a cool spring morning, and the leaves on the forest paths were soft underfoot. Leaf wanted Marian to come see the early dewdrops before they evaporated in the warmth of the sun. Truthfully, what he really wanted was to be with Marian Reed, whether the dewdrops evaporated or not.

In the first days of their friendship, Leaf had used excuses like "Miss Reed, my daughter Hetty could use a little advice about her reading." But as time passed, and Hetty was often nowhere in evidence, those invitations were recognized for what they were. Soon just the two of them began taking long morning walks before Marian had to be at her desk at the library. Then there came the frequent invitations to join the family for musical nights at the cottage. Recently he had been saying, "We would enjoy your company," without mentioning any reason whatsoever. Today he said, "You make the perfect beginning for my day, Marian. May I hope to see you?" Watching the squirrels chatter and leap from tree to tree before them, they walked for a time without the need for conversation, then . . .

"Leaf . . . "

"Yes, Marian?"

"Will we always be friends?"

He stopped and turned toward her. "We'll always be friends," he said. His gray eyes conveyed a gentle kindness.

Leaf tried to think. He must speak plainly and keep in mind her fragile feelings. He wondered exactly what her question had meant. Was it mainly about the word *always?* He looked down at Marian's upturned face, the freckled cheeks as fresh as all outdoors. Her dark brown eyes did not hold the answer.

Marian's stepfathers had been somewhat like light bulbs. Every time her mother thought the bulb might be growing dim, she replaced it with a new one that didn't last any longer. During Marian's childhood, the men were always changing. So much for the word *always*.

With his hands firmly holding her shoulders, Leaf looked down and felt warmed by her eager expression. He said, "Always."

She appeared to expect more. Marian waited, but could see he was thinking.

He watched the sun shining on the orange-red glow of her hair, and thought of all the things he would like to say, but didn't.

How could anyone leave you?

Are you afraid I'll soon be gone from your life, too? That won't happen. I don't even like to part with you when you go to the library for the day.

But maybe you want me to be like a father and fix everything. How do I explain that I don't want to be a father to you?

Maybe you think I'm too old to be anything else.

I want something more. I want to brush my teeth in the same washbasin with you, and keep my clothes in the same dresser drawers.

I wish we could sit by the fire in our pajamas and recite Robert Service poems together, with your feet in my lap.

And while I'm shaving in the morning, maybe you'd pass behind me, and when you see me in the in the mirror, you'd say, "Oops! You missed a little place on your chin!"

It doesn't matter to me whether you know how to cook. We could learn to ruin scrambled eggs together.

They continued their walk. Marian's feet felt heavy, and the unexpected disappointment she felt made a lump come into her throat. She thought about what Leaf had not said.

He was supposed to say, "No, we can be better than friends!"

I wanted him to pick me up and fling me over his shoulder, and carry me off with wedding bells ringing and tin cans clunking along behind us. Then we'd float to our honeymoon at a quaint bed and breakfast called Happily-ever-after-land, someplace halfway to the moon.

But instead, he says we'll always be friends. That was all. Friends.

What do I do now?

He loves being Hetty's father. Is it possible he wants to be like a father to me as well?

No, Leaf . . . it won't do. I don't want you to pat me on the head and say to people, "How do you like my little red-headed girl?" Or things like, "Give your best curtsey to Mrs. Ponsonbee, Marian, and thank her for the nice Betsy-Wetsy doll."

I don't want you to tweak my nose and tell me I'm cute, then go away like all the men in my mother's life.

Why can't you see I want to be your partner, to wash your socks and iron your shirts, to help you raise Hetty.

But maybe you don't see me that way.

I could learn from Dora about how to be a mother.

And just for you, I could learn to cook something besides macaroni and cheese.

Leaf felt for her hand and was puzzled when she withdrew it and walked even more slowly. Fighting the tears, she turned around and left for the comfort of the library.

Books never took her for walks on dewy mornings and spoke of friendship; they were not tall and strong, with kind gray eyes.

But she could close them when they made her unhappy.

Unraveling Like Dagwood

Morgan stopped his car at the intersection. Looking ahead through the windshield at the turbulent sky, he wondered when the clouds would lift. Although the spring weather had been unpredictable, he hoped Hetty would go up in the glider with him tomorrow. He pictured their climbing high into the sky together and could already feel her excitement at seeing the earth from above.

Morgan thought of the visit he'd had with Leaf earlier in the day.

I would never invite Hetty to go soaring without Leaf's permission. I think he appreciated my asking him.

As a father, his instincts tend to be rather cautious and protective, but I know he sees how adventure makes Hetty grow more confident. I'm glad it went as I'd hoped. He's influenced by the way Dan and Dora raised her.

When I need advice, Leaf is always generous with his time. He guides me in a way my father probably never will. But our discussion this morning seemed kind of unusual; it was almost as if our roles were reversed, and he was trying to learn something from me, instead.

He seemed to think I have my personal life all figured out. If he only knew! I'm as puzzled as Leaf is about the way women think.

Morgan smiled at the thought of being with Hetty tomorrow.

He was jolted back to reality when Katrinka addressed him. "Honeybun," she began. She sidled across the seat to sit close to him.

Morgan stared intently at the traffic light, as if all successful operations of traffic in the metropolitan area depended on his gaze. Judging from the scowl on his face, Katrinka decided Morgan was taking that responsibility very seriously.

The scowl worked. The light turned green.

Her perfume is starting to make my nose run. If we were in an airplane or a racecar, I could keep her tied in place with a lap belt.

I should've waited till this year to buy a car. Sounds like the '54 Nash is going to offer belts as built-ins. Actually, she'd never strap herself down anyway, for fear of wrinkling her skirt.

Morgan tapped his fingers on the steering wheel and thought how the average man would have preferred looking at the beautiful Katrinka instead of his own knuckles.

"Honeybun . . . " she began again.

"Yes, Katrinka?" asked Morgan, glancing sideways. She placed her left hand on the dashboard in front of him.

"Isn't that the saddest little hand you ever did see?" she asked him with a pretty pout.

"Would you like to borrow my gloves?" he offered.

She laughed her most musical little chortle and batted her lovely long lashes at him. He found himself admiring the full glory of her newest beauty product, Fanatalash, the long-lasting and lustrous mascara of the stars.

"Oh, Morgy!" she crooned. "You have such a darling sense of humor."

Morgan seemed puzzled.

Not wanting a lady's hand to remain in a state of distress, he tried once again to show his gallantry. "I'd be glad to turn on the heater," he volunteered.

Sir Galahad would have said no less, especially if it could help delay his ladyship's discussion concerning engagement rings.

Katrinka politely declined the suggestion of turning on the car heater, and for the time being she postponed speaking of her pitiful little hand with its bare ring finger.

Soon there was only the sound of the open wind vent valiantly circulating the perfume. This gave Morgan's thoughts a chance to wander.

I wonder how our marriage ceremony might read. It could be something like, "Do you, Morgy-Porgy Morganthal take Tinky-Winky Wallace to be your lawfully wedded wife to have and to hold? To be your very own ball and chain to love and to cherish, unless or until such time as she addresses you as Morgy-poo or Pookety, at which time this marriage contract will be declared null and void. Period."

Morgan decided he'd better direct his thinking toward the business matter at hand. The circus.

Katrinka wonders why we can't be more involved with our chain of banks or something nice like that. I understand why in her experience circuses would seem kind of messy. How should I break the latest news to her about having responsibility for the circus? I need to be open and direct. I'll tell her right away.

He cleared his throat.

"Katrinka, an attorney named Daniel Lawrence has been helping my father and me with some legal matters. I need to tell you about it."

"How involved can you be before you've turned twenty-one?" she asked.

"There are decisions to be made now, and they may involve you as well," he said.

"Really? This attorney, is he related to Melinda's little friend?"

"Yes. He's Hetty's father."

"How good an attorney could he be? His daughter seems a bit dim-witted, if you know what I mean."

"No. I don't know what you mean," answered Morgan.

According to Melinda, the girls at Haxton predicted that Hetty Lawrence would become an attorney. If so, she would be a good one.

"When I offered to do something about her hair," said Katrinka, "I also suggested she might need some vanishing cream, and she didn't have the foggiest idea what I was talking about."

Morgan knew people whose disappearance would make little difference to him, but Hetty was not among them. He wondered why Katrinka would want Hetty to vanish. He continued to listen.

Katrinka said, "I told Hetty she would need it to erase unsightly freckles, if she ever got any. The poor thing didn't know there was any such thing! She actually thought it was just in cartoons like *Tom and Jerry* . . . you know . . . the way they're always using it to turn invisible so they can play more tricks on each other and stuff like that."

Katrinka licked her lips, moistening her Picture-me-Pink Angel Gloss lipstick, and continued with her assessment of Hetty.

" . . . And when I told her she should brush her scalp to stimulate the hair follicles, she looked at me like she was confused, and didn't say a word. What kind of person doesn't know basic facts like that, I ask you!"

Morgan was about to confess to his own ignorance on the subject of hair follicles for the sake of honesty, when Katrinka affectionately picked an imaginary thread or lint ball from his shoulder. He gave it some thought.

Someday she might pull a real one that's actually attached to my sweater. I could end up like Dagwood Bumstead. One time he was running to catch the bus, and Blondie was still on the front porch holding the end of a thread she'd picked because it was sticking out of his sweater. By the time he caught up with the bus, he was so unraveled, all he had left on him was his underwear and a briefcase.

As Morgan had nothing of interest to add to the subject of cosmetics, he introduced a new topic.

"Later this week I'll be helping Leaf Locke move his sister's piano," he said. "Otherwise, the sun hits it this time of year, and it goes out of tune. As soon as they're through rehearsing some new pieces, you're invited to come there with me to a party."

"That's nice," she stated absently.

"Dan Lawrence will be there," he added. "It might be more comfortable for you to learn a little about the business later on, if you've met him there, first."

"Does that mean Hetty will be there too?" asked Katrinka.

"Yes. You see, Leaf Locke is her biological father. Daniel and Dora Lawrence adopted her and raised her."

"But Morgan," said Katrinka, "what a genuine mess that must be."

"Not at all."

He said it with such conviction, that Katrinka had to turn toward him and study his face. "How well do you know these people?" she asked.

Morgan's eyes were on the road. He didn't answer, because he was enjoying his thoughts.

I wish I knew all of them better. I'm happiest in the company of these people. It might be a bit early to tell Katrinka how I feel about them.

Melinda says Hetty has been planning this party and all the music specifically for Katrinka and me. I was surprised to learn how much time she and her family have spent on it. If Melinda's right, it should be a special experience.

Morgan thought of something he ought to mention.

"Are you sure you won't change your mind about going in the glider sometime?" he asked.

"You know how I feel," she purred. "I do wish you wouldn't fly. It's dangerous. Besides, I miss you so, when you're up there." Her pretty little mouth formed the best pout of her entire career.

Morgan smiled as if to acknowledge that her efforts were not entirely wasted.

"You are always invited," he said. "This morning I asked Leaf for permission to invite Melinda's friend Hetty to go up. But of course, that's only if you aren't interested," he said.

Katrinka stiffened. "Morgan Morganthal! I thought you cared about my feelings more than that. To go cavorting around the sky with that little girl. . . . What will people think! I have my pride.

"And tell me, what does this Hetty have that I don't have?"

Katrinka stopped. She had just given away her secret. She didn't think of Hetty as just a little girl, and Morgan probably didn't either.

What did Hetty have that she didn't? She had Morgan's attention, that's what she had. Maybe Hetty herself couldn't know she was now officially considered a threat.

Katrinka knew Morgan wanted her to go to Hetty's party, so this was her opportunity to strike a bargain. She blinked to hold back the tears that moistened her lovely eyes, and told him, "I'll go with you to the music party, if you'll promise never to take that Lawrence child up in a glider with you."

The Taillights of their Dreams

Leaf helped Marian over a clump of violets. He indicated a substantial log surrounded by soft moss and maidenhair ferns. "Maybe we could sit here," he said. "I'm afraid I didn't make myself clear yesterday, Marian. I was hoping we could talk a while and try to imagine the future together."

Leaf brushed the acorns off the rough bark to make it a more suitable setting for a marriage proposal.

Marian's face was radiant. She glowed with what Leaf hoped was excitement and expectation, but he thought, "I must be realistic; maybe her cheeks are just a little flushed from walking."

Leaf looked down at Marian and forgot all his well-rehearsed conversations. Her eyes were wide and eager. She smelled like the fresh air of a clear and cloudless afternoon, and he was overcome with joy at the scent of her. A blissful feeling welled up in him, blending with treasured childhood emotions.

When the clothes were washed clean, and hanging out in the breeze to dry under a bright sun, I wanted to bury my face in them. It's a smell far better than anything the tongue can taste. There is a pure sweetness that clings to the sheets so I'd want to wrap them around me and breathe in the scent. Deep in my lungs. I wanted to leap and flap the whiteness toward the sun to gather more of the clean freshness to myself.

At first, a grownup would say they've just been washed, and that we don't want to do the laundry all over again. But soon the freshness would win, and we would laugh and spin in a tangle of sheets, towels, and aprons never to be forgotten.

Leaf imagined laughing and spinning, and smelling the freshness of Marian, and then folding clothes together with her while she gathered clothespins in her apron.

They would try to keep their children from playing in the laundry. Still, it wouldn't hurt to spoil the little redheads once in a while.

Leaf didn't want to stop imagining the happiness of such an experience.

I wonder if she knows it helps to sort socks in the sunshine. If you pair them without seeing them in the light, next day someone might point out that you're wearing one brown sock and one blue one.

Actually, the idea of doing laundry might not be very appealing to Marian. Maybe she imagines spending the rest of her natural life chained to a hot and steamy washtub, or wearing her fingers to the bone as she slaves over a washboard and clothes wringer.

I'd better help her do the laundry. And I won't have her burning her hands when she irons my shirts!

Marian might be uneasy if I talk about marriage first thing before she has time to get used to the idea, so I mustn't get ahead of myself; especially if she thinks of me as sort of fatherly.

Maybe she won't think so much about our age difference if we sit together and listen to the birds a while.

It just takes patience and concentration to get birds to trust me. Then when I'm very careful and do everything right, eventually they will come very close or even land on my arm and let me feed them.

I need to do everything right with Marian, too.

Leaf heard the call of a bird and whistled in return. A bright red cardinal fluttered closer to inspect the tall plaid bird and his red-crested companion.

Leaf stretched his legs straight in front of him. Marian loved watching him as he unfolded his long legs. But then she also loved watching him when he didn't.

He's sort of like a daddy longlegs. I can hardly wait for him to be my long-legged husband, instead. I'm glad he's wearing trousers that need mending. I'll offer to patch the pocket for him after we're married.

I can tell he's going to ask me now. His eyes are already speaking to me. They are soft and deeply kind. They seem to be saying everything will happen just as it should.

I will always remember this very log and the soft green moss. This will forever be a magical place we can show our children. But they mustn't mess it up! They will have to be reverent when they come here.

I feel like saying yes before he even speaks! But I must let him say the words exactly as he has planned.

The rustle of leaves under their feet seemed almost deafening above the quiet of their unspoken thoughts. Marian closed her eyes and held her breath. How would he say it?

Leaf took a deep breath and began.

"I'm not sure how you want things to be, Marian, but I'm setting aside my pride to tell you how I feel. Ever since we met I have wanted you to be more than just a friend to Hetty."

He shuffled his feet and tactfully provided Marian with a silence in which to react to his declaration of love.

Leaf waited and hoped she would respond with something positive. It's not that he expected her to say, *Oh, my Prince Charming, at last you have come!* but the silence became unbearably long. He completely gave up hoping for a response such as, *You have made my dreams come true!* or even, *I feel the same.*

Leaf would have been content to hear, *Thank you, Leaf. I don't find you too repulsive,* or just about anything, as long as Marian wasn't laughing at him. But the only sound was the cardinal's call, and Leaf didn't notice it.

He had proposed marriage. He had opened his heart to Marian. At least he thought he had. What was he to do now?

Leaf felt somewhat wounded by her silence, but he tried to remove the mournful expression he feared was visible on his face. He would forge ahead even at the risk of further rejection.

He attempted a bright new beginning. "Hetty could use a red-headed sibling," he volunteered.

There was more silence.

Leaf tried to understand how with only six words he seemed to have so thoroughly destroyed his dreams. He had been picturing a house full of little redheaded boys and girls. Now he knew that it would never happen. Or if it did, they would certainly not have a mother named Marian Locke.

Obviously, even his mention of one redheaded child had been a mistake.

Marian too was seeing her dreams disappear. It was like she was looking at the back end of all the beautiful possibilities she had imagined only a few minutes ago, and seeing only their taillights. The lights were becoming dimmer and more distant. Leaf would soon be gone from her life like everyone she had ever cared about.

Marian's mind kept racing.

You say you want me to be more than a friend to Hetty. But pray tell me, what am I supposed to be to her? We're already dear friends. If you're asking me to be her librarian, it's a bit late for that. I've been her librarian for five years.

I want to be Hetty's mother. There's only one way to make it happen, Leaf, and you know what it is.

When you said she could use a redheaded sibling, I felt like asking who you had in mind, but of course you meant me. After all, I don't see any other redheads lurking around.

But what do you expect me to do? Share a bedroom with Hetty, so you can tuck us both into our trundle beds and sing us a lullaby? Will you turn out the lights, tell us to say our prayers and go to sleep? No, Leaf, please!

Maybe there's some reason you don't want to marry again because of your first wife. I feel as if I know Anne, and I would be honored to share you with her memory.

Being in love is supposed to make people happy, isn't it? It just makes me feel sick to my stomach.

On the other hand, my happiness depends on being near you. I suppose something would be better than nothing at all. I wonder if I can learn to be content with that.

Marian made her decision. She wasn't going to let the taillights disappear completely. She reached out to touch

Leaf's hand. The firmness of his grip surprised her. He stood and helped her up from the log.

Holding her face gently between his hands, he bent toward her freckled nose. Her large brown eyes seemed ready to overflow. Were they tears of happiness? Girls were such a mystery!

"I'm so confused," thought Marian. "Maybe I should pull away from him, but I don't want to."

"Would you give it some thought, Marian dear?" he whispered.

"I don't know, Leaf. Don't you feel like it's a little unclear what we mean to each other?"

"Is it?"

"Isn't it, Leaf?"

"Isn't it what?"

Isn't what what? Marian wondered.

CHAPTER FOUR

Remember to Yell Good and Loud

Leaf put down his violin and wandered rather aimlessly through the cottage. It was hard to concentrate on playing the Schumann selection, or anything else for that matter. It had been that way all week since his disastrous talk with Marian. He found himself sitting at the edge of his bed looking at the picture of Anne. When she was alive, she had been wise and helpful whenever they discussed their concerns. At the moment, it wasn't so much that he missed her; mostly he just needed to talk to someone. So that's exactly what he did.

I don't know what's come over me, Anne. I even miss your cold feet in the middle of my back."

"No you don't, Leaf. Not really. But you were always so nice to let me warm my feet that way," she said. "You used to holler and pretend it was a big shock," she added cheerfully.

Leaf smiled. "I wasn't pretending," he replied.

He looked out the window at nothing in particular, then decided to focus his thoughts on things that were going well—like the party Hetty was planning.

Morgan has become a good friend, and it pleases me that Annette wants to do something for his benefit. You'd like him, Anne. In fact, you'd be proud if he were a son of ours.

Her plans for the Tuesday night party are looking promising. Now she's decided on the program, it's just a matter of arranging time to practice together.

Annette's voice is unusually pure and sweet. Her range is quite good too. But the best thing of all is that she comes here to practice.

Whenever she comes, I wish I could talk to her about things, he thought.

"What do you mean, Leaf?"

Leaf could picture Anne tilting her head to listen with interest, the way she used to do when she was alive. He chose a different window from which to stare at nothing, and did so for several long minutes.

"Everything's going wrong between Marian and me."

"Are you suggesting you might want advice from our daughter?" she asked.

"Oh, certainly not! It's not like Annette needs to know there's anything between Marian and me."

Suddenly Leaf could imagine Anne shaking her head with amusement. Maybe she would even flop herself on the bed and laugh with disbelief.

"Do you really think she didn't notice you and Marian holding hands under the dishwater?" asked Anne. *"Freydis did.*

That's why she's been having you do the dishes together ever since."

Leaf's cheeks flushed, and he stroked his chin thoughtfully.

"Well," he chuckled, "I'm not really sure who I was trying to hide it from."

"Hetty may know more than you think," Anne assured him. "Besides, she would probably appreciate your confiding in her."

"You just called her Hetty," Leaf noted. "I think it might really be easier if that's what I called her, too. That is if it wouldn't hurt your feelings, Anne."

"No wonder I loved you, Leaf. Here I am, as dead as I'll ever be," she said wistfully, "and yet you're still concerned about my feelings."

"I'll always love you, Anne."

"I know, Leaf." She blinked her large brown eyes. Or was he picturing Marian's eyes? Maybe he was. Anne's eyes had been blue.

She began to float away. "I'm happy you thought marriage was good enough you want to try again," Anne said over her shoulder.

Smiling, she blew him a kiss with both hands. At least that was the way he thought he'd seen her do it a long time ago.

"If Marian's feet are cold," Anne suggested brightly, "remember to yell good and loud."

"If she'll have me," thought Leaf. "If only she'll have me."

The familiar clunking sound of elk skin boots drew near. Hetty would soon enter the cottage wearing her papa's boots.

"Father?" she called, "I brought you some cookies."

The gloom that had visited Leaf began to lift at the sound of her voice. He greeted her eagerly just inside the entrance. The bells that hung on the door chimed softly when she closed the wrought iron latch behind her.

"I've been hoping to see you about now," he said. "And to think you've even come bearing gifts," he added, looking under the flowered napkin. "Cookies . . . what could be better!"

"I just made them," she said. "I hope they're still warm."

"Oh? What kind are they?"

"I call them Tomato Surprise bars," she said.

Leaf raised his eyebrows cautiously. "I'm sure they'll be delicious," he said, trying to sound as sincere as possible.

Hetty tried unsuccessfully to keep her smile from showing.

"Actually, Father," she said, "the surprise is that there's no tomato in them."

He laughed, then the two of them sat and talked for a time over their milk and cookies.

There was another reason Hetty had come to see her father. He had seemed unusually distracted and unhappy recently. In spite of his smiles, she sensed a heavy heart. The least she could do was show him she was aware of it, even if nothing could be done.

"Where has Marian been, Father?"

Hetty watched Leaf. His eyes seemed to lose their light. They focused on a wrinkle in the flowered napkin. He folded and unfolded it, carefully smoothing the purple flowers before folding it again.

Leaf said nothing with words, but his thoughts were written all over his countenance. At last the matter had been exposed and Hetty knew why he was miserable. She wondered what to say next.

It all seems so simple. How could anything be more obvious? Why didn't I realize it before! Maybe it's because Marian is such a fun friend, and I couldn't see past that. I thought she just liked to be with all of us so she'd have sort of a family.

She looks all dreamy-eyed at Father.

Does he think she's too young?

I can see it all clearly now: Father doesn't speak openly, and Marian will always be afraid of getting hurt, so she won't take a chance.

It's not my place to say what I think. I shouldn't meddle. Maybe people need to make mistakes on their own.

Hetty sighed to signal a change of thought.

"I was supposed to meet Melinda after school," she said. "At three-fifteen under the clock tower. That was our plan. So I watched the spot where we were supposed to meet, the whole time. I kept looking from around the corner to see if she was there or not. While I was doing that, she was waiting around the *other* corner so she could see me when I got there. That whole time, neither of us actually went there, so finally we both gave up and went home."

"Funny how people do that," said Leaf. He poured another two inches of milk in their glasses.

"I know," said Hetty. "I always think something like that can just work out, but it doesn't unless I make it happen."

Leaf looked out the window. There were some little groups of gnats that kept dancing up about three feet above the grass, then another group would go up in a little swarm and trade places with the first. They went on for some time getting nowhere, just moving around in their little circles then trading places. He wondered about them for a while.

Do they sometimes bump into each other, but mostly just go up and down until they die? Maybe they do like Marian and me. We might bump into each other off and on, and say how are you? Oh, fine, I'm enjoying going around in stupid little circles, sometimes up, sometimes down, sometimes sideways. I'm enjoying my meaningless little life, thank you. I hope you're having a delightful time getting nowhere, too.

Marian's not a very good cook. If Hetty shared her recipe for Tomato Surprise bars, she might actually add tomatoes to them, but I wouldn't mind. Marian could put pickles in them and I would love them anyway.

Leaf looked down at the plate that had once held the cookies. "I think they were very good," he said, wondering if he would ever have a cookie made by Marian. "What do you think?"

"What do I think?" asked Hetty. "I think you should say something to her like, 'I love you very much, and will you marry me.'"

Hetty suddenly had his full attention. If the little gnats were still dancing around, they went entirely unnoticed.

"Just like that?" he asked in wide-eyed surprise.

Hetty tried to look absorbed in gathering crumbs. "That's what I think," she replied.

Leaf didn't have to debate with himself. He knew Hetty was right.

Suddenly, everything gave him pleasure: his empty glass, with its miraculously-even coating of milk on the inside, sitting so gracefully next to the artfully scattered cookie crumbs; the pearly gleam of the milk where it gathered ever so slightly more thickly toward the bottom of the glass; the scratch on the table, which transformed the surface into one of such mellow beauty that he wondered how it could have escaped his notice in the past.

His head swirled with excitement. Stretching his arms high, he threw back his head and laughed.

"Of course. What a fool I've been! I should have said those very words!" He drummed the table with both hands.

"I'll take a dozen red roses with me . . . or maybe yellow. I want to see her right away.

"Maybe she'll have me, Hetty!"

Leaf spun Hetty around in the kitchen and thanked her with an enthusiastic squeeze. Then with a wink in her direction, he was out the door.

Vargo the Magnificent

Of course she'll have you, Father, Hetty thought with confidence.

The idea of having Marian in the family was a new and happy idea to Hetty. It was the perfect thing to savor high in the branches of Hannah. She ran along the path to the great oak and climbed the thick vines to her perch where she could mull it over in her mind.

Hetty was almost bursting with things to enjoy. The circus was in town, and Melinda had actually invited Hetty to go with her on the opening night!

It surprised Hetty that Melinda seemed almost businesslike about the event, when she herself found it so exciting. Then she thought about it.

Ever since I heard a real elephant came to Melinda's birthday party once, I've wondered if anything in her entire life could seem that exciting to her again.

Maybe Morgan will drive us there! He'll smile so it makes his eyes kind of crinkle at the edges, then clap his hands and say, "Let's go, girls!"

If he drives, I hope Melinda will sit next to him so I can sit behind her. That way, I can see him from the back. If I had to sit next to him, I wouldn't be able to watch him, because he'd notice.

His hair is thick and really dark brown. And his eyebrows are heavy and make him look kind of serious. When his sleeves are rolled up, I like to see how the hairs on his arms are dark to match. Maybe he has to shave the back of his neck every day where his hair grows down inside his collar. I wonder if it's scratchy.

I have him all memorized.

If Morgan ever got amnesia because of an accident—like if his glider crashed or something like that—I'd probably know about it by instinct. I would look everywhere for him, until finally I'd find him in a hospital in some place like Nepal or the Belgian Congo. All the nurses will say he is the most tragic case they have ever seen . . . that their hearts ache for the handsome and courteous young man who doesn't know anything or anyone from his entire past.

He'll be looking out the window of his room. When I come up to him from behind, all I'll be able to see is the back of his neck. But I'll know him, for sure.

Even if he doesn't remember what's happened to him, and doesn't know his own name, when I run over to him, our eyes will meet, and he'll say, "I knew you would find me, Hetty."

When we get back home, and he's completely better, he'll say, "I don't know what we would have done without you, Hetty! Katrinka has been so worried about me! You've saved the day."

Katrinka will say, "You found him just in time, so we won't have to change our plans or even cancel the wedding cake we ordered."

She'll tell me that when the baker puts the little figures of the bride and groom on the top of their cake, there will be a third figure.

Katrinka will say, "You see, we want him to put one of you on it, too, dear Hetty, because you're the one who has made it all possible!"

On the day of the circus, Hetty was disappointed to see a black limousine pull up the long driveway toward the Lawrence home, because it meant Morgan wasn't the one driving them to the circus.

While Melinda came up the front stairs to ring Hetty's doorbell, the driver was so short he disappeared when he went around the back of the car. When he reappeared and opened the door for them she was surprised his only claim to height was the tall hat he wore down over his brow.

As they approached him, Melinda said, "This is Phil." Phil smiled when Hetty reached down to offer her hand. He doffed his hat, which made him appear a fraction of his original size. After he mounted a stepping stool to reach his place on a high driver's seat, Hetty noticed the car was cleverly outfitted for his use.

While their car wound down the driveway, Melinda said to him, "I bet Hetty's never met a real, live clown before." She turned to Hetty. "Have you?" she asked.

She didn't wait for an answer. "Phil's a clown. A really good one," she said, "but he's having back trouble, so he's on leave from the circus for now. He's Katrinka's dad. They're both staying at our place, in the gatehouse."

Phil glanced over his shoulder at Hetty. "I believe you're the young lady Marian Reed tells me about."

Hetty remembered Marian speaking of a friend named Phil. "Oh, that's right! I remember she told me you know a lot about elephants in America," she said.

It was fun talking with Phil, and Hetty was sorry when the conversation ended. As the Morganthals lived on a large estate, she had never met Phil, but knew Melinda and Morgan both had a high opinion of him.

After Phil left the girls at the entrance, Melinda led Hetty by the hand through the crowd. They made their way to a front row seat. A barker with a tall purple hat and matching megaphone leapt into the spotlight.

The surroundings were pleasantly chaotic. The wide-eyed little girl next to them was aware of nothing but the sequins on the blue and gold vest her parents had bought for her. The chubby toddler behind them could see only his own noisemaker that threw sparks as it smashed into his neighbors' hats.

How could anyone find something like that and concentrate on just that one thing to the exclusion of everything else? Hetty wondered about it.

I love watching the trapeze artists, the way they make it look so easy to fly through the air. Still, I wouldn't want to choose just one thing to watch. I might miss the silly costumes or the smell of popcorn and cotton candy.

I'm surprised the only thing Melinda seems to care about is whatever new act might be coming next. Instead of watching

*the ones already performing in front of us, she just keeps both
eyes on the entrance.*

Hetty was watching a poodle act off to the left. She
cheered when the smallest dog leapt over the others, with a
gigantic foam rubber bone it had stolen from the largest one.
Melinda didn't notice. She had finally found something to
interest her. It was *Vargo the Magnificent.*

The mysterious Vargo made his entrance to the fanfare
of trumpets. Riding into the ring on a snow-white horse, he
seemed to glow in the spotlight. A string of six more white
horses pranced after him, white plumes waving high over
their heads.

Except for his gold riding gloves and a red cape that
billowed behind him, he was dressed all in white. Even though
the mask he wore was white like the rest of his costume, he
made Hetty think of the Lone Ranger. Melinda never took
her eyes from him as he rode his horse around the ring.

When the poodles leapt out of the spotlights, Hetty
decided the horse performance was the main attraction.

As Vargo and the horses continued to circle, Hetty
noticed a man who had been crouching on the sawdust floor
in the middle of the ring. He snapped a long whip to lash at
the nervous animals. They were doing an impressive job of
looking frightened, so it made an exciting show.

The horse Vargo was riding reared up on its hind legs,
pawing the air as if to defend himself. As its front hoofs struck
the floor, a shock of dark hair fell forward over Vargo's mask.
Gripping the saddle with his gloves, he balanced briefly on his
hands then arched his back to gracefully dismount. Once he
was in the ring, Melinda became more involved in the drama

of the show than before. She stood and called to Vargo, "No! No! Don't do it! Look out!

In spite of Melinda's anxious warnings, Vargo wrestled the man to the ground and jerked the whip from his hands. The crowd cheered at the fast-moving show. At that instant, the lights in the ring went off.

Hetty's attention was drawn to her right, where she watched twin clowns drive a tractor between the legs of an Uncle Sam on stilts, but Melinda continued to watch the darkened ring and the nearby exit. For some time, she seemed to have her mind on Vargo the Magnificent.

The crowd thinned and the lights dimmed. The magic that was once the circus now littered the floor. Stepping over spilled popcorn and discarded candy wrappers, the two girls made their way to the front entrance where Phil was waiting for them.

Hetty heard him speak to Melinda under his breath. It sounded like he was saying, "It was barbed. Morgan's all right."

The drive home was quiet. Phil allowed Melinda's private thoughts to go uninterrupted, and Hetty did the same. Something had happened that she didn't understand.

Hetty thought about the front row seats they'd had at the circus, and her mind wandered.

I bet when the Morganthals want to go to a concert, the conductor of the London Symphony comes to get them in a whole ocean liner, like the Queen Elizabeth *or something, and gives them a private performance in the dining room while they eat truffles found in the forests of France by a pig wearing a beret.*

When they go to a football game, the coach himself probably picks them up at their front door. Then maybe the team members

*run up from the end zone during the game into the stands to
give them free hot dogs with everything on them.*

Cuticle Care

"Daddy . . ." began Katrinka.

"Yes, Trink?" Phil put down his fountain pen and gave her
his undivided attention.

"Morgan hasn't talked about a wedding date." She paused,
then added, "I've hinted all I can about an engagement ring.
I think maybe he's interested in someone else. Things aren't
going the way I expected."

"Max and I have thought for years you and Morgan would
be a match made in heaven," he smiled. "Max even used to
say Morgan could only inherit his money if he married you."

Phil laughed. He thought briefly about that. Max couldn't
have meant it. Or could he?

"Does Morgan know how you feel about him?" he asked.
"With the number of boyfriends you've always had, maybe he
doesn't know he's special to you."

Katrinka thought maybe it worked both ways. She
remembered once when she was with Morgan and a group
of flirting girls swarmed around him like flies. She would have
used a flyswatter to scatter them, if she'd had one. Morgan had
been attentive to her alone, but his attention did not seem
as sincere as she would have liked. It was more as if he were
using her as the flyswatter instead.

When Katrinka looked back on that annoying event, she
pictured herself perched daintily on Morgan's shoulders, a
diamond tiara in her hair. It flashed with sparks to ward off all
the flirty girls.

She pictured her fingernails finally grown out all to the same length. After careful attention to her cuticles, she imagined her nails painted with a really aggressive-looking deep blood-red nail polish and an extra coat of lustrous long-lasting nail protector. She would point her fingernails at the crowd to make them cower and melt like the plastic doll she had once left on a hot radiator.

While they were all slinking away, Prince Morgan would wrap his purple velvet cloak around her and whisper in her ear that she was the most gorgeous female human being upon the face of the earth, and he couldn't wait to start pampering her. He would say she was so special to him that he hadn't noticed anyone else was there.

Not even Hetty Lawrence!

But if he had noticed her, she hoped Morgan might have seen Hetty hadn't even bothered to push back her cuticles.

Katrinka sighed. "Morgan just told me his father's been given the circus to run," she said. "I wish you'd told me, Daddy."

"It's better for the two of you to talk these things out yourselves, Trink," he answered.

She sighed. "How much responsibility do you think Morgan will have?"

"Please don't worry, honey," he said gently. "Over the years I've been preparing him to handle whatever comes, and I believe his father will soon be capable of taking more on his shoulders."

As much as she hated the circus, Katrinka was grateful it had provided a living for her father. So many people with dwarfism had trouble finding work. Katrinka was glad for her father's lifelong friendship with Maximilian Morganthal and his family. And it was a relief to know Max was getting help with his drinking problem.

Katrinka removed her shoes, then peeled off her Fanatalash-enhanced eyelashes and put them in their case.

If there was one thing she had learned from her father, it was how to make the best of a situation when you can't change it. It would do no good to wish things were different. Still, she longed for those years of her childhood before her mother had died, before she had been sent away to school.

"I've missed you so much, Daddy!"

He took a long look at Katrinka. It didn't seem appropriate to tell her how sweet she looked now that her eyes were her very own. Not now. He held his tongue, and thought about it.

Instead of being taken as a compliment, it might sound judgmental to her.

Maybe she's trying to hide her insecure feelings with make-up. Ever since her first year in college, Katrinka's been acting slightly affected and artificial the way she talks with other people.

I hope she's able to be her real self when she's with Morgan. He is fine and good. Can I trust him to know that she is too? He may have to look beyond her act.

"It hasn't been the same without you," he replied.

"I know," she said. She stood behind his chair and began working with her fingers to knead his neck and shoulders. He hummed with appreciation.

"I wasn't merely referring to your excellent back rubs," he laughed.

Katrinka leaned forward to rest her cheek against his, and said, "I know, Daddy."

The Lump

Leaf couldn't see Marian soon enough! He ran across the library parking lot with the roses cradled in his arms and hurried toward the glass entry of the building. Always before, the door had opened easily. This time it wouldn't open!

Oh, maybe it was because he was pushing. It was clearly marked, *Pull to open*. He laughed at his own befuddlement.

Through the door he could see Marian standing next to her desk. She had her back to him and was speaking to a young man. Leaf chose not to interrupt their animated conversation.

To Leaf's surprise, after a while the fellow put his jacket around Marian and they left through the back door.

However long it might take, Leaf would await her return. Nothing was about to stop him from following through with his plan!

He approached Marian's desk to admired a fresh bouquet of pink and white roses on the ink blotter. Tucked in it was a gift card signed by a sure hand in bold letters. It said, *I can't believe I've found you! Love, Joseph*.

The assistant librarian saw Leaf waiting, and told him Marian had gone home feeling sick. Leaf sat down to consider what it all meant.

"There seems to be someone else in her life," he thought. "Maybe she won't have me after all. I'll have to wait for her to feel better, then I'll find out."

A day later, Leaf carried the wilted yellow roses up Marian's front porch, and hoped Marian wouldn't notice how floppy their heads had become. Waiting had seemed unbearably long. He looked at the gift card that poked pitifully through the cellophane. Across the top it said, *Congratulations on your graduation.*

That was the only card the florist could give him, other than *With Profound Sympathy*, or *Happy Groundhog Day*. It hadn't mattered to him at the time, but now he wished it looked more assertive, and that his hand hadn't been trembling when he signed it.

Leaf wasn't quite ready to ring the doorbell. He had some thinking to do, and once he crossed her threshold, that opportunity would be lost forever.

Her young man might be confident and smooth. Maybe he's the kind who wears spats and gives Marian perfume that he's had mixed to his own specifications by a team of French fashion designers.

But if Marian is ill, maybe she would prefer someone fatherly. She knows me as someone she's used to and doesn't need to impress. I'll be to her whatever she wants.

Leaf had just steeled himself to knock when he noticed the door was already ajar. He heard nothing, but looking in through the crack, he saw a lump on the couch.

The lump might be his dear Marian. Leaf ran to her side and folded down the top of the quilt. The girl of his dreams had a little piece of tissue clinging to one nostril. Although she was shivering, her hair was matted with perspiration and stuck to her face. She lay curled around a pan. Whatever it was she had eaten earlier for lunch—perhaps a chicken salad or deviled eggs—apparently she feared it might soon reappear.

One white sock and one striped one were sticking out from under the blanket that she had pulled up under her chin.

He heard a low moan, which to his ears sounded like, *Oh, what a blessing that you have come to rescue me in my hour of desperate need!*

In reality, the correct interpretation was, *I would rather die than ever have you see me this way!*

He tucked the covers around her feet and blotted her damp forehead with his handkerchief.

A glass of water had spilled on the carpet, and the water pitcher was empty. When he visited the kitchen sink to refill the water pitcher, there was not enough space to do so, until he had washed the food-caked dishes that were overflowing the sink. While he was washing them in hot soapy water, Leaf remembered when he had held Marian's hand under the dishwater.

Suddenly it occurred to him that the young man who had given her the flowers might come to pay a call. If he were someone Marian cared about, she would be embarrassed to have him find her in such horrendous surroundings! He hurried back to the front hall to gather up miscellaneous tools, a wastebasket, clothes and canned goods that appeared to be waiting for the next trip to the garage.

His years of being a bachelor hadn't prepared Leaf to launder a lady's unmentionables; however, the laundry basket was piled high, and Leaf imagined Marian would soon be wearing a barrel if he did not do a few washloads.

He returned to see how she was feeling. Her face had taken on a greenish hue. She squeaked something he took to mean, *Thank you for taking such good care of me. I couldn't ask for a finer father figure. How kind of you to come to my rescue! Because of you, I won't be humiliated when Joseph, my new suitor, comes to ask for my hand. Will you give me away when we are wed?*

In reality she was saying, *Here comes my lunch*.

It had been an accurate prediction. Leaf supported her head over the pan. When Marian said she felt a little better thank you, Leaf disposed of the contents. He returned to kneel at the side of the couch.

Leaf looked at her beautiful greenish complexion; her lovely bloodshot eyes with the sunken gray circles, and he knew the magic moment was now. In a flood of emotions, Hetty's words came to him.

"Marian," he said, " I love you. Will you marry me?"

CHAPTER FIVE

The Slightest Hope

Morgan Morganthal entered the law office of Daniel Lawrence. Dora greeted him warmly, took his coat, and offered him a seat in the broad leather armchair.

She offered him one of her homemade oatmeal cookies. "We enjoy your sister Melinda," she said. "Hetty finds her such good company."

Some untidy wisps of hair had escaped, and Morgan watched her tuck them under the thick braid that framed her small face. Morgan smiled at Dora. He waited quietly and hoped for any possible reference to himself.

He waited in vain.

Surely if Hetty felt any affection for me at all, she would have spoken of it to her mother.

Maybe I should mention Hetty again in case it just didn't come into her mind to say anything at first.

"It's so thoughtful of Hetty to be planning that musical program for us," said Morgan. "I'm amazed that she would do such a thing!"

Dora's eyes twinkled. "It would be hard for you two to find a more effective matchmaker than Hetty," she laughed.

Morgan puzzled over Hetty's eagerness to tighten his relationship with Katrinka. It was almost as if she looked on his engagement as a sort of mission.

The smile on his lips faded, in spite of his efforts to keep it in place.

What else could I expect? Hetty could never care for me! Even if she did, she's far too young to be promised to anyone.

For that matter, maybe I am too. How can I be so close to getting engaged? It was complicated the way I got into this situation.

If I had any chance with Hetty, I would wait.

She'd never be happy without a good education—that's always been important to her whole family—and she won't finish college for at least another five years.

Still, I would wait for her.

An ancient love story came into Morgan's thoughts:

It took seven long years of waiting and laboring before Jacob earned the right to marry Rachel. Then it was another seven years after that before she really became his.

The difference is that Rachel wanted him to wait. The only reason Jacob felt like the years passed quickly was that he knew she loved him in return.

I'm a patient man, but I would need to know there's hope . . . even the slightest hope.

When the door into Dan's office creaked open, Morgan thanked Dora for the cookie and entered the pleasantly cluttered office. Books and papers were piled precariously in the most unexpected places, yet they gave Morgan the confidence that worthwhile and creative thinking would soon take place.

Closing the door as quietly as possible, Dora smiled at her husband through the crack. She watched as Dan greeted his client and brushed cookie crumbs from his book of Constitutional Law onto Morgan's trousers. Morgan pretended not to notice.

Dora sat back behind her desk and considered the young man with the serious dark blue eyes. The crease between his eyebrows seemed to reflect a heavy concern.

I hope Dan can help lighten some of Morgan's burdens.

Leaf says he took on a lot of responsibility early in life. He's met his challenges well, but it's meant missing out on the typical carefree experiences of youth.

Hetty's childhood certainly wasn't typical or traditional either. It couldn't have been, since her health was so fragile in those early years.

Have we made a mistake sending her to an all-girls' school? Hetty doesn't seem interested in boys yet. Marian's brother Joseph is nice enough, but he can't get her attention. Some of the girls at her school seem a bit overly interested.

Of course, it's because she hasn't gotten to know any very well. Hetty is bound to take an interest as soon as she sees that there are some fine ones. Like Morgan Morganthal, for instance.

The Morganthal family's wealth has had little effect on Morgan—except, as Leaf says, to give him an awareness of how little connection there is between money and character.

I wonder—while he still has some time, before he gets married, if he might be willing to be a big brother to Hetty. It might help if she saw someone like him as a role model. She needs to know what attributes to look for in a man, when the time comes.

Maybe he'd be kind enough to pay her a little attention. I think Leaf could find a way to ask him.

The Care and Keeping of Elephants

In Dan's office, Morgan's legal issues received the thoughtful consideration he had expected.

Dan leaned back in his chair and put his feet up on his desk. "Maybe you should give me a little background to begin with. Go back as far as you feel is necessary," he added.

"My father was unable to come," said Morgan, "but it may not matter." He paused while Dan honked his nose melodically into a large handkerchief.

"Our primary concern is for the safety and fair treatment of the animals," said Morgan, "but there is also the fear that since I discovered and exposed their mistreatment, there may be some publicity that could damage the reputation of the circus. If it should affect the success of the show, a lot of people we employ would suffer."

"Tell me about the management of the circus up to now," said Dan.

"The man behind the operation has been Phil Wallace. Phil and my father grew up together, and he's been like an uncle to me. When I've needed to get away from home, I've stayed with Phil in his trailer."

Dan knew Phil was the father of Katrinka Wallace and that he would be invited to Hetty's music program. "That's how you know Katrinka?"

"Well, I don't know her as well as I might." Morgan looked at the floor, and wondered what Dan thought of his answer. He breathed deeply and continued to explain. "Phil has always been a loyal friend, and I feel indebted to him for all he's taught me.

"After his wife died," continued Morgan, " Phil sent Katrinka to boarding school. He felt she would have a better future if she were away from him. Her mother died when she was young, from causes related to her dwarfism. And Phil's health is poor. Also, he wanted to spare Katrinka some of the humiliation he's gone through," continued Morgan.

"He began as a carpet clown, and worked his way up from there."

"Carpet clown?" Dan raised his eyebrows with interest.

Morgan shifted his weight and continued. "The circus mostly consisted of trained animal acts in the early years. The mud in the ring had to be covered with a carpet between acts, and the audience would get restless while it was being spread out. The solution was to have clowns lay it out in an entertaining way, with pratfalls and so on.

"Later on they worked the audience. Mingled with people in the bleachers. Phil and my father were a very successful act. Being complete opposites made them even funnier together. My father was the tall, quiet one. Phil had a gift for involving strangers in the action.

"Phil tells how one night, when they were working the bleachers, Dad met the boss's daughter. Dad sat on her date's lap pretending to powder his nose with a powder puff the size of a bathmat. In the laughter and confusion, her glasses got caught in his wig and they broke. When he followed up to make amends, they fell in love. That ended the clown act." Morgan paused and smiled. "Now you know how my parents met.

"I imagine my father would be clowning with Phil even today, if my mother didn't object. Apparently Dad's an amazing juggler and magician, but I've never seen him do anything of the sort." Morgan looked at the crumbs on the carpet. "I've never known him to be really happy," he said.

"Phil has stayed on as an executive, but my father hasn't been entrusted with responsibility for any of the businesses. That is until now. I'm sure it's been somewhat disappointing for him all these years. Finally he has something to look forward to.

"It was Phil who suspected our elephant trainer was abusing the animals. He was right. I caught the man with unnecessary barbs on his whip.

"The man told me the use of gaff hooks is standard —necessary for controlling the elephants. We were just beginning to investigate, when Phil suspected something was wrong about the horses, too.

"The trainer told us everybody does it, but my father said, 'Well, we don't!'"

Morgan thought with pride of his father's determination. "My father isn't afraid of bad publicity," Morgan added. "He just wants to do the right thing for the animals."

When Maximilian Morganthal had toured the elephant cages, Morgan saw a side of his father that he never expected.

"My father and I would both prefer it if animals were able to remain in their natural surroundings," he said. "Dad told me that he once watched a baby elephant being separated from its mother. It was being sold to another circus. He could never bring himself to ask about how the baby was doing, but the memory of the mother crying out for her baby has stayed with him.

"My father and I want to be fair with the trainer's innocent family. Also, I suppose if we should fire him, he might retaliate. He could take out his revenge on the animals."

Dan had an idea—one that would solve not only Morgan's problem, but a concern of his own as well. He honked his nose into his handkerchief and took his feet off the desk to face Morgan squarely.

"Maybe you and your father don't really want to have elephants in the show anymore. The problem of firing the animal trainer will simply evaporate if the job no longer exists. If you should both agree on it, you have enough land on your estate to help you phase them out. Until the elephants have been placed to your satisfaction, couldn't you keep them there?"

When Dan suggested the possibility, Morgan was surprised.

"Our elephants are the biggest draw, so we've never considered phasing them out," he replied.

Dan looked deep into the blue of Morgan's eyes. "You need to take a hard look at what you want and make sure it's the right choice. Decide if it's worth the price you have to pay," he said. "If it is, then pay it."

Morgan's eyes were steady and solemn, as he took a hard look.

What do I really want? I want to be with Hetty. I want to sit high in Hannah and know I am welcome there . . . that

I belong in her world where there are gentle words and kind thoughts. I want to hear her sing to me alone, with her pure and sweet voice. To see her smile with her eyes, just at me.

I want to sit with her and watch while she whittles her pencils into totem poles. I want to fly with her. We can rise up higher, to where there is more and more light and we can dream of the beautiful possibilities before us. Together, I think we can do anything.

That's what I want.

Dan was surprised and pleased at the happiness he saw in Morgan's eyes. The idea of letting the elephants go seemed to be a bigger relief to Morgan than Dan could have imagined. Maybe his plan had possibilities, so he kept mulling it over.

Maybe Morgan wouldn't mind having Hetty help him with the care of the elephants if they should decide to keep them on their estate. She has good instincts in caring for animals. She's a lot like Leaf that way.

Morgan is recognizing the good in Max now. I like his attitude, and I'd like Hetty to learn from him.

She may not want to. After all, she still prefers to be alone most of the time.

Hetty hasn't taken much notice of boys, and it's about time she learn to get acquainted with one in a comfortable way. That is if it wouldn't be imposing on Morgan.

Leaf and Morgan have become good friends. I wonder if Leaf could find a tactful way to ask him.

The corners of Morgan's eyes crinkled into a smile. He said, "I wonder if our property is zoned for elephants."

No Answer

Hetty cradled the baby chimpanzee as it slurped milk from a baby bottle. It pulled Hetty's hair and felt her cheeks. Hetty laughed as it explored her nose with a hairy little hand. Morgan and his father Maximilian stood outside the pen and watched from a distance.

Within ten days of Morgan's conversation with Dan, the animal pens had been installed on the Morganthal property, and a satisfactory routine would soon be established.

In spite of all Max and Morgan had said to prepare Hetty, she was surprised to find almost as much came out the tail end of an elephant as they fed into the trunk end. Hetty was as quick with the shovel as the men were, and just as willing.

"I don't think we're paying Hetty enough," said Max. "She's more than pulling her weight. How did you happen to hire her?"

Morgan folded his arms.

"Well, she's not too involved socially. Leaf wanted her to have a chance to . . . how do I say it?" Morgan paused to move the hose, and began again. "I think he wanted me to sort of take her under my wing. Mainly because everyone else she knows is a girl, and I'm not. I really don't mind doing it."

"I can see you don't. I'm not blind."

Once again Morgan's eyes were drawn toward Hetty. The happy chimp was bonking the empty bottle against her head.

Morgan decided it would be best to appear less interested, and he forced himself to look down at nothing in particular.

Max was the first to break the silence that followed. "Melinda is missing a lot by going to summer school. She would have loved being in on the fun."

Morgan thought of the sign Hetty had made for the inside of the elephant pen. Blossom often startled people by spraying water on them with her playful trunk, so Hetty made a sign to forbid it. The sign said *Elephantos omnis admonet: Ne aqua populus unda.* When he asked her why it was in Latin, Hetty had said, *It might as well be. Elephants can't read English anyway.*

Morgan smiled to see Hetty rocking the contented little chimpanzee. It snuggled against her neck. He deliberately looked away to clear his thinking.

Facing his father, Morgan said, "Katrinka won't even come look at the animals, Dad."

Max looked into space and tried to calculate the length of time Morgan and Katrinka had been considered engaged. He wondered if it would ever really be an official engagement; if so, would that period also be tiresomely long and drawn out?

"What's been holding you up, Morgan?"

Morgan countered with another question, one he had never before dared to ask his father. "Why is this so important to you? Why Katrinka?"

Max clenched his jaw; Morgan's question should never have happened, and it would not be answered. "You don't need to know," was his firm answer.

Max cracked his knuckles. "I've resented your getting involved where it's no concern of yours." He gave Morgan a stern look. "You took over Melinda when she was our responsibility."

Morgan thought of how neglected his sister would have been without his attention, and felt his anger rising. But rather than let it show, he stopped to consider what Hetty might do if she were in his position. He remembered something that had happened the previous week.

*Hetty had just sprayed Blossom
thoroughly with the hose.*

Morgan and Hetty had been cleaning the elephant pen when the driver of the hay wagon came to deliver feed. Blossom swayed with excitement and flapped her ears. Her hay was coming!

The driver seemed surprisingly uninterested in the exuberant elephant; however, when Hetty and Morgan approached him, Hetty got his attention. He eyed her up and down and said, "Man, ain't she a tall one!"

He shoved the invoice through the truck window at Morgan, and said to Hetty, "Least ways you're not near as funny lookin' as some skinny girls."

Morgan had felt inclined to punch him in the nose, but before he could make known his anger, Hetty smiled and thanked the man.

If there were two ways to take something, Hetty took it the best way.

Morgan decided to take his father's remarks the best way, and held his tongue. Then he faced his father squarely and said, "It's a pleasure to have Melinda for a sister."

Max was not accustomed to paying compliments to his son, but he realized Melinda was becoming a fine young woman, and the credit lay almost entirely with Morgan.

It took Max a while to form the words.

"You've done well, son."

The Tightrope

"Morgan?"

"Yes, Hetty?"

"I wish this summer would never end."

Morgan said nothing. He mustn't face Hetty directly, for fear she would recognize the warmth of his emotions. Instead, he looked over at Blossom and concentrated on the flapping of her ears. She was the last elephant needing placement in a new home.

Earlier in the month Barnaby, the younger bull elephant, had been delivered to the old mahout who had been reluctant to part with him in the first place. Barnaby left while he still had the sweet honeycomb smell characteristic of young bull elephants. Now they wouldn't have to endure his destructive frenzy and the rancid odor he would emit later, during his seasons of musth.

There were no plans yet for the baby chimpanzee.

Hetty admired Morgan's gentle persuasive way with the animals. He and his father had formed a bond, though cautiously at first, based upon their shared concern for the elephants. It had been a surprise to see Maximilian Morganthal so involved in the details of their care.

Morgan, Max, and Hetty had to learn how to put a healing salve in Blossom's eyes. It had taken all three of them to do it safely. Max had seemed distant and stern in the beginning, but Hetty no longer considered him unapproachable. The Morganthals were beginning to feel more like a family.

Hetty had just sprayed Blossom thoroughly with the hose, and the steam was now rising from the happy elephant's back. She swayed contentedly while waving her trunk like a conductor before an imaginary orchestra.

"Let's move into the shade for a few minutes," said Morgan. They locked the pen and sat down on the lawn under a young maple tree. The grass felt cool and pleasantly soft.

Hetty asked Morgan about something she had suspected. "Did Papa talk to you about getting me to help you here?" She became quiet while he considered his answer.

"No, he didn't," said Morgan.

He soon reconsidered his response. It had been a half-truth, and he decided to make it into a whole one.

"It was Leaf," he said. "Why do you wonder?"

"Because I didn't think you would have asked me otherwise," she said. "The way Father brought it up, would you have felt free to turn him down?"

"Of course." he replied.

Morgan looked at Hetty's sky-blue eyes and the soft pink of her cheeks, and he could hardly breathe.

Closing his eyes, he thought back to his conversation with Leaf Locke.

Leaf came to me almost apologetically . . . unsure how I might answer him. Yet if I had dared, I would have gone to him myself, begging for this time with Hetty! Leaf provided me with the excuse I could never have dreamed of. He has entrusted her to me with the understanding that I am promised to someone else. He believes my feelings toward Hetty are those of a big brother.

He is a good friend, as well as Hetty's father. I mustn't take advantage of the situation in which he's placed her.

Hetty explained the involvement of her parents.

"Mother and Papa have always tried to get me to socialize. They want me to be comfortable mixing with people.

"When I was twelve," she said, "I was afraid to go to the library for fear I might have to talk to the librarian. Can you imagine anyone being afraid of Marian Reed?"

Hetty folded her hands together as if to say that had been the final chapter of her extreme shyness. She quickly took a breath and opened a new subject. "Did Leaf tell you he and Marian are getting married?"

"Yes, but if he hadn't said anything, I would have guessed it anyway. He seems so changed and excited."

"Is that the way it is when you're happy—like with you and Katrinka?"

Morgan pretended an urgent need to search through the grass at that exact moment.

Maybe I could look for a four-leaf clover. Surely there must be one around here somewhere! It probably won't be hard to find one among the trillions of ordinary ones. Not hard at all, compared to telling Hetty I'm planning a marriage that shouldn't happen.

I feel like I'm a tightrope walker in a high wind, and Hetty is the one person encouraging the others to cheer for me. Up here on this rope, all I can think of is falling, and I want to turn back.

Just because I've almost reached the far end of the tightrope, is that a good enough reason to keep going? I've tried so hard to imagine having things work out with Katrinka. If I can't make myself go through with it, I'll disappoint a lot of people: Mom and Dad, Melinda, Phil, and Katrinka.

And there's Hetty.

I mustn't disappoint Hetty. She needs to see me as steadfast and loyal to Katrinka. Wouldn't Leaf and the Lawrences want Hetty to see those qualities in me, too?

That's why I can't turn back. Yet Hetty's the reason I want to.

Morgan didn't find what he was looking for in the grass, but a better diversion occurred to him.

"Dan has given me a lot of helpful advice about the business, but he's also helped me think through some of my career plans," said Morgan. "There's so much practical use for a law degree. What would you think if I were to go to law school?"

"How does Katrinka feel about it?" asked Hetty.

"It's your opinion I want, Hetty."

Hetty grew quiet. She looked up through the leaves and tried to see the clouds, but they seemed too distant.

"When I close my eyes I can see you flying," she said softly. The next words were almost whispered. "Maybe it's because you seem so far above other people in my thoughts."

Morgan dared a glance at her. She was using the corner of her sleeve to wipe something from her eye.

His mind raced with his hopes: *Maybe she isn't so committed to linking me with Katrinka.*

Please, Hetty, he thought, *oh, please tell me what you want!*

"Anything you choose to do you'll do well," she continued, "so I will always see you that way, whatever your decision may be."

Hetty brushed her hand over the grass, and Morgan wondered if she might be looking for the same four-leaf clover that had eluded him.

"Leaf admired my Uncle John, who was an attorney. I never knew him," she said. "Leaf thinks I should consider law school, but I'd probably be the only girl there. There weren't any women in Papa's graduating class."

Hetty continued. "Actually, I wonder if the reason Father thought of the law school idea is so I can find a husband. What I could do is stand up in class the first day and say, 'Hi, everyone. I'm only pretending to be interested in the law. I'm really here so I won't be an old maid. I'm looking for someone who doesn't care if I'm tall as they are.'"

Hetty paused briefly and thought, "To be honest, I'd have to tell the class I'm shopping around for another Morgan Morganthal, since the one I want is taken."

She thought back to the sensitivity of the ideas she had just laid bare before him, and blushed.

Morgan clenched his fist and tried to laugh. He thought, "Why is she saying these things? If she just wants me to joke with her, that's what I'll do.

"We could be law partners," he stated. "I can just see 'Lawrence and Morganthal' in the front window."

"We could have fun dividing up our specialties," she said. "You could specialize in sports torts."

"Or maybe witness fitness," he laughed.

"You'd be a great deposition magician," Hetty added.

"And you could take on the erroneous felonious cases," laughed Morgan.

Hetty clapped her hands and said, "We could work together on surgery perjury!"

All this silliness had provided relief from the fear of their disappearing dreams.

Hetty cocked her head and tried to read Morgan's suddenly serious expression. "Really though," she said, "you'd be so good at helping people think through their problems. It's rather fun to imagine. And if we had important things to talk about, I can picture our sitting up in Hannah to think them through together."

A smile of joy and relief began to crinkle the corners of Morgan's deep blue eyes. *She must feel I belong with her in Hannah,* he thought. He looked up through the lacy leaves, and suddenly the bright sky seemed to beckon him to take Hetty by the hand—to fly with her above the pure whiteness of the clouds.

Morgan thought of the time spent with Hetty this summer. He couldn't remember happiness like that ever before. Perhaps it was the gentle wisdom she had learned at home; Hetty had been the bridge uniting him with his father in small and cheerful ways. Morgan's happiness had nothing to do with Katrinka.

He remembered what Dan had said: *Take a hard look at what you want; make sure it's right. Decide if it's worth the price. If it is, pay it.* Morgan was ready to pay it and hoped Hetty would want to pay the price too. Maybe she understood his feelings for her now. Surely she would want him to climb down from his tightrope to be with her.

Hetty looked at the green space between them, and thought,

I love this lawn, because I'm sharing it with Morgan. We're not far apart. The distance seems even smaller because of how we can speak with each other so comfortably. Maybe it's because we think alike about so many things that matter to us.

But not everything! I really don't understand how it can matter which football team wins. It seems like you should be excited about what any of the players do, if only they try hard enough.

I don't mind at all the way Morgan laughed when I told him that. I guess it's one of the mysterious things about men that I'll never understand. I loved seeing him whoop and holler with his dad when their favorite team won. Melinda even joined in, and she doesn't know any more about it than I do.

Hetty breathed deeply with contentment. She would enjoy being with Morgan while she could. She would memorize the feeling, then try to forget it.

She thought, *Morgan is too honorable to show interest in me even if he wanted to. Maybe he should know I admire that.*

Hetty began. "One reason I love you. . . . " She paused, searching for another way to say what she had in mind. "I meant to say, one reason I love the way you are with Katrinka is because of your loyalty.

"I love seeing how happy you've been this summer while you're going about making it happen."

"Is that really what you want, Hetty? To see me make it happen?" He smiled.

Morgan was unprepared for her response.

"Oh, yes!" It came from Hetty with so much conviction it startled him.

Her firm answer was intended to hide the sickening heaviness that welled up inside her.

The sky seemed to darken. Morgan looked absently at the grass, and his dark hair fell across his forehead. He felt choked by an unspoken disappointment that hung in the air.

Blossom was still conducting her imaginary orchestra. She swayed rhythmically, waving a stick she gripped in her trunk.

Her message seemed to be, *Move on with your life.*

CHAPTER SIX

The Special Number Five

Oh, Hannah, I'm ready to burst with feelings of I don't know what. Last night was our music night, and after we finished, Mr. Morganthal wanted to take a picture of us all together with his Polaroid Land Camera.

When Morgan and Katrinka stood together they looked so perfect that I thought they ought to be on a Valentine card. The kind with cupids flying around holding hearts attached to little swags that drape over them so they appear modest enough that the artist doesn't have to ruin the picture by putting diapers on them.

They looked absolutely made for each other.

So here's what happened: Mr. Morganthal had me stand next to Leaf for the picture because he was the only person taller than I am. He certainly couldn't put me right behind Morgan and Katrinka. It would detract from the two of them, since I'm about half an inch taller than Morgan, with my shoes on.

In glee club, I usually have a solo part, and it makes sense for me to stand in the middle of the back row. But for this picture, there was no easy way to place everybody.

We carried in some chairs we thought could be useful. That way Phil's face was level with Katrinka's when he sat next to her. But the way we kept worrying about who should pose where—such a flurry was made over our various heights, that it became sort of laughable.

So guess who fixed everything. Morgan did.

He said it wouldn't matter where we put anyone, except for me. He said the real reason he and Katrinka had such a wonderful night was because of my organizing the program.

The next thing that happened was Morgan put his arm around my waist and brought me to the front row to stand between him and Katrinka. He said lots of nice things to thank everybody who did anything, and best of all, he kept his arm around me while he did it. He stayed next to me like that until his father had taken five entire photographs. That means five will always be a special number for me.

I'd gone over to Melinda's earlier, and while I was there Morgan made me some sketches to explain an idea he has. He wants to use a kind of slingshot to get his glider off the ground. That way, he won't need to have a car tow him when he's trying to take off.

I want to learn all about thermals and how to find them. So I asked him about when warmer air expands, and what happens when it gets so it's less dense than the air around it. He explained about thermal columns and some other amazing things.

Even if he never takes me up in his glider, I can pretend to myself that he has. All I have to do is think of the number five, and I'll imagine I'm soaring with Morgan. I can dream we're rising high over the windward side of a beautiful green slope. We'll follow what he calls a cloud street and glide together toward a ridge where we can lift with a warm and steady wind.

I could have listened to Morgan talk that way forever. I only left because Melinda said it was time to go.

In all the time I was there, Morgan never mentioned my going gliding with him. I've decided he must not want me along, or else he would have.

When we left Morgan, Melinda and I went straight to the gatehouse. We met Katrinka so she could try to tame my hair before the program. That's when I found out she agrees with me about the importance of keeping promises.

I told her she and Morgan looked like the absolute dream couple, and how Melinda and I had vowed to do whatever we could to help her and Morgan be ecstatically happy. She told me she knows Morgan keeps his promises. It's a quality she admires in a person.

Katrinka doesn't think Morgan will be taking me flying.

It took about two hundred hairpins before Katrinka got my hairdo the way she wanted it. After she was all through, she instructed me not to go outside, in case the wind would muss it up. As long as I didn't, Melinda said she had a guarantee to proclaim: I would definitely look like a possible addition to somebody's harem.

Katrinka brought me a mirror, and called to her father in the next room so he could see too. Phil stopped what he was doing and came to admire her work. He declared it was the most amazing and clever head of hair he had ever seen in his whole entire life, not counting the phony ones he used to wear in the circus, that were made out of yarn and styrofoam.

Next he said we ought to take a photograph of it. That way I would have a picture to keep forever to remember how gorgeous Trink had made my hair look.

Katrinka could see how that might be good.

Phil said I might be able to sing better, however, if I looked like my real self.

She looked at him and got really quiet.

He also said, "Natural is good," and he wondered if I was more likely to be at my best if I didn't have to adjust to being so terrifically elegant.

I could have hugged him on the spot!

Katrinka took out all two hundred hairpins. It was a lot of work, and she was a really good sport about it.

I'm trying really hard to like her for Morgan's sake.

You know how some people can't help acting the way their Halloween costumes make them look? By the time I got back to the cottage, I looked like me again, which may not be all that great, but at least I didn't have to worry that I'd automatically turn into somebody like Rita Hayworth while I'm singing, "Oh, Promise Me."

There's not much to say for the tangles in my hair, except they're mine.

One time our class went on a field trip, and Sue walked into some low-hanging branches. Her hair looked like she'd combed it with an eggbeater, and Gretchen said, "You have Hetty hair!"

It's kind of fun, because now whenever somebody's hair goes wild, they bring their heads over next to mine to get compared.

Anyway, I felt prepared for the program, and it went pretty smoothly. When you are looking into faces of people you love, things usually turn out all right.

It's sometimes hard to predict how group singing is going to work, but that part went well too. I stood up in front to hold up the words for people to see. Father played the harmonica while everybody sang "The Sweetheart of Sigma Chi" to Katrinka.

Mr. Morganthal has a really wonderful voice. Leaf took him off to the side and talked to him. He came back by the piano and sang "Some Enchanted Evening." After that, Father invited him to sing with us some other Tuesday night. I don't think Melinda and Morgan had ever heard him sing before. It must have been fun for him to see how surprised and proud they were.

I could tell Mr. Morganthal liked Melinda's headmistress. His wife would have been impressed too, if she'd come and met Aunt Freydis.

During the group singing, Mother went to the kitchen to fix the refreshments. Afterwards, she brought out the most beautiful little heart-shaped cakes. They had a filling of almond paste and homemade strawberry jam. Some even had wafers poked into the icing to look like butterfly wings.

Absolutely nobody could believe she made the fortune cookies! Of all the fortunes Papa and I made up, my favorite one said, "This is a piece of paper. Do not eat." Another was a strip of paper that said, "The future lies ahead." For the rest of them, Marian had found some sentimental sayings.

Father told us Marian couldn't come because she had food poisoning.

I keep thinking about something that happened. It was a sort of feeling that came over me. We were singing, "Don't Sit Under the Apple Tree with Anyone Else But Me."

Oh, Hannah . . . it's hard to explain, but I got a lump in my throat. I realized Morgan might not ever sit here with me again.

He is the main person who makes me want to be my best. It seems like when I try to look at things through his eyes I know what's important instead of what only seems important . . . like the way he helps Melinda look for the best in their parents and find things to admire about them.

When we finished the song, I remembered something that happened five or six years ago. Even though I was just twelve years old when we met, Morgan stood up for me when I entered the room. I was nobody at all, and yet he made me feel like I was important.

I must keep remembering how he makes me reach toward being better. That's something I'll always need to hold onto. I wonder, Hannah . . . would it be right to forget such a friend?

Marian read me something by Elizabeth Bibesco. She says, "To others we are not ourselves but performers in their lives cast for a part we do not even know we are playing."

I don't think I should tell Morgan how great a part he plays in my life. He'll be Katrinka's inspiration, and he'll help her have the vision of all her possibilities. They can lift each other, and reach together for everything that's fine and good. I won't be any part of it.

Maybe I need to pretend to myself like Morgan's dead.

Still, there are things I shouldn't let go of—like trying to understand things through his eyes. Maybe nobody's really dead till we forget them.

Sometimes Father likes to imagine talking to Anne. He says it helps him to think, when he has her point of view in mind. After she died giving birth to me, Leaf thought there would never be anyone else. But like Mother and Papa say, "There's enough love to go around, and exercising it doesn't use it up."

I guess some people see friends like those steel inertia balls where you pop two down on the left side and it sends two flying off the right side. I don't want to bump off one person to make room for another.

I think maybe it isn't Morgan I need to pretend doesn't exist. It's the number five. It would be wise to bury the number five.

"Hetty?" It was Morgan looking up at her from the forest floor. "That was a beautiful night," he said.

Hetty's eyes were on him, but she didn't invite him to come closer. He began again.

"We had spoken about gliding. I need to explain. I'm so sorry, Hetty," he said. "I won't be able to take you."

"I know," Hetty said. "It's Katrinka you need to take."

Hetty thought of the verse, *Oh, promise me that someday you and I will take our love together to some sky. . . .* She had sung those words to Morgan and Katrinka.

"She'll want to go up with you, to see you flying . . . to soar with you and to love you in the sky the way she loves you everywhere. It'll be a memory she will treasure forever."

Soft puffs of Hetty's hair floated before her eyes, but they couldn't hide the tears that began to gather.

"The clouds will always remind her of you," she said.

The clouds will always remind her of you

There was a catch in her throat. It felt like the number five was jumping up and down saying, *Ha, ha! You didn't bury me as well as you thought.*

Morgan grew thoughtful. Shaking his head, he said only, "Hetty, Hetty!"

She looked down at Morgan's shock of dark hair and noticed the graceful arch of his back. The sun fell on him, making him glow as he had under the spotlights at the circus.

Vargo the Magnificent had been Morgan!

The Cotton Candy Mistake

The next morning, Morgan's steps were slow and heavy to match the weight of his thoughts. As he walked to the kitchen, he was determined to invent a positive plan.

Maybe the time will pass better if I think of ways to get to know Katrinka, he thought. We ought to adjust to one another before we continue. I can't see many places our goals match, so I'll need to work at it.

Here we are, planning the wedding for only a few weeks away, yet I haven't felt committed enough to give her a ring.

Morgan gazed at the distant trees. *If only I could interest Katrinka in flying,* he thought. He watched the trees sway in the wind. He wondered where Hetty was. Could she be watching them too? If she saw the silver leaves shimmering in the wind, would they make her happy?

Hetty's face floated through his mind; her image was always there. Morgan remembered her visible emotions: the tears she was trying to hide as she spoke of his flying with Katrinka, the soft puffs of her hair and the glow of her cheeks.

Does she know what she wants?

Actually, he thought, *she's young, and probably fickle like my sister Melinda.*

When Melinda was five, I took enough money to the circus to buy something for both of us. Melinda wanted pink cotton candy at the snack booth, because it was the very first thing she saw. The other booths weren't open yet.

I waited till they had all opened. When I'd seen everything that was available, I bought a bird you could whirl overhead on a stick. It sounded like pigeons do when they first take off flying.

After that Melinda thought everything else looked better than her candy; even the mug that looked like an elephant's foot. I had to give her my bird so she'd stop crying.

Maybe that's how Hetty is, too. If I take her to the soda fountain, maybe she'll want a root beer float till she sees the cherry phosphate in the next booth. When the cherry phosphate comes, she'll ask if she can change her order, because the hot fudge sundae looks far better.

Of course I'll give her anything she wants.

But I can't take a chance on her choosing me just because I'm the first thing she sees.

Normally Morgan liked a good hearty breakfast. The cook had gone for the morning, so Melinda had heated up a cold slab of ham, and he fried their usual four eggs.

While waiting for the toast to pop up, Melinda tried to reach Hetty by phone. The line was busy.

"I wonder if she has a boyfriend. She's probably talking to Joseph. I can't ever get through to her," she complained.

Morgan felt stunned. Suddenly the idea of eating made him feel sick, and he left the eggs as they were, staring up at him from the plate. He thought about Marian's stepbrother Joseph.

Joseph might suddenly sweep her off her feet. Maybe Hetty can picture a storybook future with him. He's tall and impressive. Is that what it takes? No, I don't think so.

But she might get sort of used to him, if he keeps taking her dancing. Maybe that would be enough for her . . . coasting along through life, just being used to each other.

No, Hetty Lawrence isn't the coasting kind. She wants to make good things happen. She'll always take the road that goes up, and there's no such thing as coasting uphill.

Hetty makes me want to be at my best. I wonder if she has the same effect on Joseph.

Morgan made himself push the greasy eggs around on his plate as he thought.

Maybe all Joseph has to do is something simple. He might hand her an empty candy wrapper and say something ordinary like, 'Don't say I never gave you anything,' and she'll smile.

Then he'll wink at her and she'll laugh the quiet way she sometimes does when she kind of ducks her head and her eyes twinkle.

Maybe she'll always remember that moment, and forever she'll do like Joseph said; she won't say he never gave her anything. Even if he never remembers her birthday or their anniversary. Even if that candy wrapper is the only thing he ever gives her.

That's the way Hetty is. She'd never make anything of it.

"I won't stand for it," Morgan muttered. "I won't let her be unhappy!"

Melinda was surprised to see Morgan slam his fist into his open palm. "He'd better be good to her," he said.

Imagination

Hetty dragged herself to Hannah where she could talk freely and climbed to a comfortable branch. Her thoughts were in turmoil.

Oh, Hannah . . . I haven't told my parents or Leaf how I feel. It seems all wrong. Especially since I've always been able to talk to them in the past.

I guess we've all been pretending I'm too young to care for anyone special. I don't think they're ready for that to change, and I haven't wanted it to, either. But it did. Maybe they sort of want me to stay a child, and I haven't wanted to disappoint them.

I like believing in Santa Claus, and I will my entire life! I always help Mother wrap the presents, and then next morning, we all say, "Well, well, Santa must use the same paper we have at our house!" Then we run outside to look for reindeer hoofs, and if there aren't any prints remotely like Donner and Blitzen would have made, I like to sneak out and make hoof prints on a piece of cardboard to show them.

Santa always leaves a love note to thank us for the cookies and hot chocolate we've left by the chimney. Papa usually tells Mother how good they were, so I let him know I'm terribly impressed by how he can read Santa's mind.

Still, I can't believe what I did . . . the way I lied to Morgan. I told him I'm eager for his marriage to take place so he'll be happy. Now he thinks that's what I want to see.

Papa says either we can stand by like observers or we can make things happen. So now I have to choose what to do about my lie. Should I make it unhappen? Or should I just stand by?

Actually, by doing nothing to correct it, I'll be keeping the promise I made with Melinda. After I spoiled Morgan's pre-engagement party, I told her I'd help Morgan and Katrinka be happy together. It's been a long time since then.

Papa would give me good advice, if I could tell him. But I can't. I wouldn't want him to think it was Morgan's fault for making me feel the way I do.

Maybe my imagination is to blame. I can wish Morgan cared for me, and I can keep looking for reindeer tracks, but imagination won't make either of them suddenly become true.

I should be grateful for the concern my family feels for me.

They always try to help me socialize. After I'm through working with the animals, Marian's stepbrother Joseph sometimes goes to the movies with us.

Joseph never gives up inviting me to do things, and it's nice of him to ask. He's a good dancer, and he's very tall. Sometimes I enjoy him, but when I do, it's because I'm pretending he's Morgan.

I think the reason we go on picnics a lot is because Marian can assemble a pretty good sandwich. She has trouble with cooking, but assembling goes pretty well. Actually, I'm not afraid to swallow the things she makes, like I used to be.

Leaf does a lot of the cooking, but when he eats her food, no matter how bad it is, he finds something nice to say. One time he told her the catsup she had served was especially good. That will not be remembered as his most convincing compliment!

Marian said, "Uh oh. The honeymoon's over," and they laughed so hard they could hardly eat. At least that was their excuse.

After redirecting her thoughts, Hetty felt just a little better.

Walking slowly home, she arrived at her house shortly before supper, closed the door to her room, and lay quietly on the bed.

Dora said she would save a portion of pot roast for her, in case her appetite should return.

Hetty pulled a scratchy woolen afghan up under her chin, feeling it was all the comfort she deserved. She stared at the ceiling.

In my old room, before the tornado, I could look up at a whole bunch of interesting cracks. My imagination turned them into lots of different pictures. I could see Indian princesses riding painted ponies, and things like that.

I used to imagine I saw the route where Sacagawea guided Lewis and Clark across the country.

When she was doing all that and translating for the men, she was younger than I am. Next to the light fixture is where I figure she was reunited with her brother.

She and the men were in the teepee of a really important chief, and she was translating for the men by firelight. They were trying to bargain for food and horses because their situation was absolutely desperate.

They weren't having any success until suddenly Sacagawea realized the chief was her brother. She hadn't seen him since the time she was kidnapped as a small child.

She stopped and wrapped her own blanket over his shoulders. It was a symbolic gesture that he alone understood. It was an absolutely magic moment, and it probably saved their lives.

Maybe I'm supposed to stop letting my imagination get me in trouble. Is that why I don't get to have cracks on my ceiling anymore?

I'd better stop imagining altogether. When I look at my oatmeal, it's supposed to look like oatmeal. Oatmeal is oatmeal. You shouldn't expect it to be a desert island teeming with cannibals or wild boars, depending on what the raisins look like.

Someday, I'll be on a drab street corner, surrounded by stray mongrels. They'll be barking and sniffing at the oatmeal I'm hiding under the orange crate that serves as my seat. That's all I have to live on and to feed my orphaned chimpanzee for the whole week. That's the only reason I don't share it with the dogs.

This scratchy blanket is my most treasured possession, even though it's infested with fleas. I'll be huddled over a fire I've made from burning the remaining scraps of my cedar hope chest—the one Papa and I built when we thought there was hope someday I would marry.

A dark-haired stranger approaches from the shadows to ask directions to a hotel where he can water his horses. His elegantly dressed wife has smooth yet wavy hair, and a poofy thing in the back that defies gravity. He turns briefly toward her. Suddenly the northern lights illuminate the sky with unimaginable splendor, revealing the graceful arch of his back and the dark hairs where his white starched collar touches his neck.

I know that neck! I memorized it long ago for just such a moment as this. For one brief instant, the stranger's dark blue eyes penetrate my own, and I see they are enlivened by tiny flecks of brown.

Do I detect a flicker of recognition? Yes. He turns toward his wife.

"Trinky-dink, I would like you to meet Hetty," he says. "Her name is short for Heliotrope." Gallantly removing his hat, he faces me and inquires whether that is not correct.

"Actually, it's short for Henrietta."

"I'm so sorry, Henrietta."

"You needn't be sorry. It hasn't been so bad. Over a lifetime, there have been other sorrows to surpass it."

"In truth, Henrietta, I'm referring not to my name but to my own mistaken recollection."

His wife curtseys, and behind her pink satin gloves, she whispers, "Morgy-poo, you really shouldn't speak with strange women. Not when you're such an important and famous attorney."

He pays no heed. Reaching into his pocket, he finds a diamond studded card case his wife had given him for their twentieth anniversary. The card he removes says, Law firm of Lawrence and Morganthal. Morgan Morganthal, Esquire. Specializing in sports torts.

"I practice alone," he explains as he presses it into my trembling hand. "The name 'Lawrence' is in memory of someone I sort of knew long ago."

He continues to puzzle over my identity. I stand and remove my afghan, which I have kept wrapped tightly around me to prevent chilblains, whatever those are. It is the one possession I treasure.

I bend over and place it around his shoulders.

He bows deeply.

As he walks off into the sunset, I see him hesitate. He gazes longingly into the sky at the birds soaring above the clouds then turns for one last look in my direction.

He pretends not to notice the fleas.

Prune As Required

The trellis arching over the front gate was laden with late-blooming roses. Marian had arrived at the cottage earlier that morning to help Leaf with the pruning of it. The cuts had to be made the right way.

She had learned how to do it by studying diagrams in a library book. If done wrong, the cultivated plant could revert back to the scruffy, undisciplined natural state of its wild parent plant.

Marian's attention to details was a source of pride for Leaf. How quickly she had become something of an expert! He appreciated her eagerness to please him.

"Are you sure you would like to live here after we're married, Marian?" he asked. "We could find a home of our own, if you prefer."

She smiled. "I'm going to love living here at the cottage, Leaf." This was the answer Leaf had expected.

"Besides," she said, "if Hetty spends half her time with Dan and Dora, I want to be around whenever she comes here. Otherwise, I'm afraid we'll miss her terribly.

"Another thing," she said. "Joseph could stay on at my house until we sell it. The way my brother's enjoying Hetty, I think he'd like to find a job here instead of going back to Australia.

"But are you sure Freydis won't mind if we stay here at the cottage?" she asked. "I know it's a tight space. Morgan says he can help us bring the double bed down from the attic." She spoke with enthusiasm.

Leaf was pleased. He was going to love having Marian's youthful eagerness around him all the time. "Thank you, Marian dear," he said. "I had hoped you would be comfortable with that for now. And I'm glad we won't be missing Hetty's last year at home before college."

Leaf knew Freydis and Hetty thrived on their time together. He had marveled at their close and comfortable companionship in the kitchen. It was even better when Dora came for their recitals on Tuesday nights, and he knew they would welcome Marian as well.

Marian was relieved beyond all imagining. She had been wondering how she could ever learn to make a pleasant home for Leaf without the influence of Freydis and Hetty.

Marian's face suddenly looked somber. She became so quiet that Leaf wondered if she was reconsidering her answer.

The words came rapidly. "I'm scared, Leaf. I don't feel ready for this. It's going to be for keeps. It's not going to be like it is for Hetty, the way she can have a toothbrush at both houses. I'll be here full-time and you'll be stuck with me forever.

"And I'm frightened that I'll be a horrible mother. What if we have a baby that doesn't look exactly like you so it seems like a total stranger and I'll have to act like I love it!"

Leaf wasn't worried in the least. He knew even a mother hippopotamus or warthog instinctively loves its young. However he felt it best to take the matter seriously.

"I can see you're frightened, Marian. If such a blessed event should occur, we'll just take it one day at a time," he said calmly. "I'm glad you're sharing your worries with me. I love you, Marian."

She looked up into his eyes. Maybe there was no reason to worry. For several years, she had been tending a little girl named Gorilla. Marian's only connection with Gorilla was that Camilla, her mother, was a good friend. The funny little child was not easy to care for, nor was she related. Yet Marian loved her dearly.

Marian felt comforted by Leaf's gentle response. At the same time, his words had highlighted a difference between them. Leaf had used the expression *a blessed event*. That's what she called *getting pregnant*. Leaf considered his first wife Anne to be *formerly alive*. Marian considered her just plain *dead*. She wondered just how much these little things mattered. Not too much, she hoped.

The trouble is whether I'm prepared for this, she thought. *For three years my preparation has just been practicing writing the name 'Marian Locke' hundreds of times. Hetty's more mature than I am.*

The sweet-smelling breeze from the forest reminded them both of the many pleasant walks the two of them had taken there. They pruned the roses on the trellis and trimmed back the bishop's weed along the cobblestone path. Deep in thought, they continued to work alongside each other, preparing the garden for their wedding reception.

Marian thought, *All I can do is my best. If I keep pruning myself correctly, maybe I won't revert to being my mother.*

Leaf was occupied with wondering how he could be so blessed. Marian would become his wife tomorrow.

CHAPTER SEVEN

Beyond the Creaking Door

The evening shadows were lengthening. Hetty had absently held her violin under her chin for quite some time before she slowly placed it back on the piano bench. She almost feared the playing of it would prove all music had died in her.

The birds seemed to carry on as usual, however. They twittered noisily from their roost in the ivy over the front door. Hetty sighed. If they could sense the thickness of gloom surrounding her, would they continue their chirping?

Suddenly something unsettling happened to silence them. A shadow crossed the window, and they fluttered away in alarm.

A scuffling, then all was quiet. Hetty stiffened.

Maybe a knock would soon happen. She waited and listened to her own shallow breathing. Time itself seemed confused. Either it was forever or just minutes; she wasn't sure which. Years ago her fear of the dark had confused time, but she must not be afraid now. No, it wasn't dark yet.

She was alone in the cottage. That meant she had to move alone past the window then alone to the front door.

The moment she turned the light switch, the lamp in the front hall burned out with a ping that seemed to devour what little light had been there. She must gather her courage to face whatever it was, before hearing a knock.

The knock never came. Pulling the wrought iron latch, Hetty made her ears concentrate on whatever sounds would come next; the creaking of the door, the tinkling of the bells that further advertised someone's invasion.

Hetty blinked at the glare beyond the open door and sucked in the outside air.

There stood Katrinka. "Ah, Hetty," she said, "I've come to show you something! I wanted you to see it before anybody else. Because I owe you so much."

Katrinka kept her hands behind her back. "You're such a doll, Hetty! Melinda tells me you both made a promise to help Morgan and me. I'll confess, I really didn't know you were sincerely . . . I mean I never thanked you properly for the party. When Morgan told me how happy you'd be about our engagement, it made all the difference."

Then Katrinka daintily extended her left hand. "I should've warned you to put on your sunglasses!" She winked and tilted her chin up ever so slightly to give herself the queenly advantage over Hetty. It was unlikely that Hetty would ever flaunt a diamond of such magnificence.

When she felt sure Hetty had been sufficiently dazzled by her engagement ring, Katrinka continued. "This is the one I've had picked out for over eight months. I about gave up hope he was going to give it to me." Katrinka smiled sweetly. "I know it's silly, but I thought there might be someone else. Maybe even you!

"Isn't that hysterical?"

Her words all ran nervously together. "Everybody says we look perfect together," said Katrinka. "I'm going to have an all pink wedding. It's all decided.

"And wait till you see my dress! It has an extra long train. Max thinks my bridesmaids will need a lot of rehearsals, so they'll know how to carry it.

"I hope all those smelly animals will be off the property in time for the wedding," she said.

"Oh, by the way, you know why Morgan got me such a big diamond? It's because I'm the reason he'll inherit lots of money." Her chin went up again. "I mean he only gets it if he marries *me!*" she said. "Isn't that fantastic?

"Obviously anybody else would be a fool to go after him," she said. Her tone was confidential. "Because that would make him be poor, you know. Everybody knows Morgan couldn't give up being rich."

Katrinka licked her lips to make them glisten. Then she was gone.

Hetty stared at the empty space where Katrinka had stood. The color drained from her face, and she steadied herself against the doorjamb. Tomorrow, she would go to Hannah.

She Can't Make Me Believe It

Oh, Hannah, I need to be with you! You are just what you seem and I can always count on you.

What if Morgan isn't what I thought? How can I ever again trust my mind and heart?

Somehow, it hurts if I have to feel disappointed in him . . . like he died long ago and I couldn't see it. Maybe the way I wanted him to be wasn't there anyway, and what's left now is the real Morgan . . . the one I don't recognize.

It shouldn't be this hard to lose a friend. Especially if he wasn't one in the first place. But it is.

Melinda used to say Morgan didn't care so much about things his father bought for him; mostly he wanted Max to spend time with him. She thinks deep down he admires his father.

Another thing Melinda said was that Morgan wanted to prove he didn't need his father's money. And that's why he worked as a smokejumper to put himself through college. Was it more for the adventure? It never seemed like he cared that much about money. But now if he had to give it up, maybe he couldn't.

I've been foolish and childish to suppose he loved me. He's never once said he did.

Still, it's hard to let go of all the good things I used to imagine about him. I can still look for the qualities I admired.

Can I find them in someone else someday?

Hannah seemed unconvinced. When the stately oak remained still and quiet, Hetty realized it wasn't merely because she was a tree. It was because of how preposterous her own rambling statements had been. She redirected her thoughts. This time with honesty.

I don't know what's the matter with me, Hannah. I wasn't thinking straight. I said those things because I'm worried for Morgan and I can't cry any more.

Everything seemed dark to me last night because I was so afraid. Somehow I knew it would be Katrinka at the door, and I could picture myself giving up.

Morgan once told me how he could avoid feeling fear when he jumped from the plane. When they'd get to a raging fire, the Ford tri-motor would circle to find the best place to drop the men. When the parachutes were packed just right and their tools were sharpened, Morgan would mostly just be eager to get down there and put the fire out. That's because they were prepared.

Morgan said that's how I could chase away my fears too.

Sometimes all I had to do was picture his face and it made me want to study harder for an exam. I've never told him he's the reason I've done so well in school.

Anyway, I need to prepare my thinking. I'm in charge of my own thoughts. Katrinka's not. She can't make me into a victim staring at the headlights. I have better things to do.

Katrinka can tell whatever story she wants, but she can't make me believe it.

It Doesn't Work that Way

The next evening Phil looked out the window at the moon that illuminated the Morganthal estate. He cast his gaze across the vast expanse of manicured lawns and sculpture gardens. He put down his fountain pen and closed the ledger.

Where was Morgan? For years, the boy had called on Phil with regularity. Strangely, now that Katrinka was here, his visits had become quite scarce. Wouldn't he even open wedding presents with her?

Katrinka sat on a little stool in front of him wearing her wedding veil. Wrapping paper cluttered the floor of the gatehouse and a few of the wedding gifts she had previously opened were on the coffee table before her.

Katrinka surprised him with a question. "Do you love me, Daddy? Tell me you love me!" she cried.

"You know I do," Phil answered with concern. "You're everything to me, Trink. What's the matter?"

"What if I've done something awful?" she sobbed.

"No matter what you've done, I will always love you," he assured her. "Whatever happens, honey."

Phil waited patiently to hear what troubled her. However, she took a few minutes to compose herself.

Katrinka had never given Phil or his wife a moment's trouble, unless he counted a few long-distance calls from the high school where she was boarding. The principal had suggested Phil might urge Katrinka to be less generous with her kisses. Maybe a firm letter would help. Phil had replied that she was simply blessed with a sweet, affectionate nature.

He held her at arms' length to look into her eyes. That way, she would know to be straightforward with him.

Her lip quivered and her eyes filled with tears. "Why can't you make Morgan love me?"

Phil put his arms around her. His heart ached with a father's concern.

She sniffed and continued. "I just wanted Hetty to see that Morgan wanted me most of all, so I showed her we're engaged. Then I tried to make it so she wouldn't like Morgan any more," she said mournfully.

"What do you mean by that, honey?

"Well, I told her how he'll only get his inheritance if he marries *me,* like you said." She blinked her long, lovely eyelashes. "And that he wouldn't want to be poor.

"Daddy, do you think that's why he's marrying me?"

Phil was speechless. If that was the reason, it would never do! Morgan would have to adore her for her wonderful qualities. Katrinka was his treasure, and could not be bought for any price.

"There will be no inheritance," he said firmly. "I'll see to that."

Phil resolved to speak to Max tomorrow.

Katrinka blew her nose and looked puzzled. "But Daddy, suppose he does marry me just for the money. At least that way there's a chance he'll like me in the future. If there's no future, there's no chance."

"It doesn't work that way, Trink," he replied.

He smiled and took her hand in his. Secretly, Phil realized she had a point, but he said, "Morgan will have to prove to me you are the girl of his dreams, or I'm not giving you away."

He reviewed with her the moment of incredible joy when she had been born twenty-four years earlier.

"You can't imagine our emotions," he said. "We could hardly believe our eyes! Never has a baby been so perfect. It was clear right away. We fully expected you to be formed like us. In fact your mother and I actually wondered if they'd brought the wrong baby to her in the hospital room." He chuckled. "We had to keep looking at you."

Phil paused. "I should never have sent you away to school," he said. "You needed to do your growing up here at home."

Phil thought of the many ways she still needed to mature. "There's something you might keep in mind," he said. "From what I've seen of Hetty Lawrence, she could be a good friend. You'll feel happier with yourself if you are kind to her." Katrinka couldn't look directly into her father's eyes.

"Think you can find a way to make it up to her?" he asked.

Katrinka had to focus her eyes on the floor until she could change the topic.

Her voice was uncertain. "When I see how sweet Morgan is with Melinda," she said, "I can tell he's a lot like you. I've always wanted to find someone like you, Daddy. Except I don't want him to have anything to do with the circus."

"Well, that's because you had to put up with children teasing you about your parents," said Phil. "It'll be different now," he said, "and I won't be around too long."

Phil decided not to reveal his health problems to her just yet, and he returned to the earlier subject.

"Morgan has always been involved with the circus," he said. "He picked up tumbling easily when he was a youngster. And everything else I taught him. Now he's just as quick to learn the business end of it. I'm afraid you'll need to get used to it."

Phil thought of Morgan. He was a fine young man, and his development was a source of well-deserved pride for Phil. Morgan was the son he would have wanted.

"The circus will be his business from now on, honey." He took her in his arms.

"Please, Daddy," she pleaded, "can't you make him love me?"

Her shoulders shook as she sobbed. Even the tenderness of her father's words could not console her.

You Didn't Know Which End

As Leaf entered the cottage, he was greeted by his wife's beaming smile and the question, "What do you think?"

Marian was indicating something in the general direction of the dining room.

Whatever he was supposed to notice was not immediately evident to Leaf. He took a chance on the tall vase of flowers in the center of the table. Initially, the only compliment he could think of was that they were stem-side-down in the water. His wife was bright-eyed with expectation, so it was a relief when an answer came to him.

"They're a wonderful color of pink!" he exclaimed.

"Nature handled that part," she laughed. "I was talking about the way I arranged them."

Her face was radiant with joy. Leaf couldn't help observing how well nature had handled the creation of Marian, and he said so.

Dinner was soon on the table. Marian poured water in the drinking glasses and watched as Hetty and Freydis made final preparations. Observing them was both inspiring and overwhelming. However did they do it!

The Lawrences arrived and as the family began to find their usual seats, Joseph knocked on the door. For the time being he was staying in Marian's old house. Joseph was just in time to find a seat between Hetty and his sister Marian.

In order to see around the immense centerpiece of pinkness, they all had to wobble and stretch their necks. Even so, the effort did nothing to dampen their lively enjoyment of one another.

Soon the conversation was in praise of the salad Dora had provided. Marian was aware of being the only female at the table who hadn't prepared anything for the meal. Unless pouring the ice water counted for something. The ice cubes had clung obstinately to the bottom of the pitcher until the entire clump decided to let go, splashing onto the lip of the glass and shattering on the tablecloth. But it happened only two times, and she knew where to get a dishtowel with which to blot it up.

She said, "My mother always told me if you can read, you can cook. I've discovered it doesn't work that way. I can read, so I thought I'd just bring home *The Joy of Cooking* one time from the library, and that would take care of it for life. It didn't."

Marian glanced at Hetty, suggesting the special advice was for her benefit.

"You're doing fine, Marian!" came the encouraging and somewhat sincere chorus of voices. It was known by everyone there that Marian had not grown up with the expectation of marrying, so her homemaking skills were getting a late start.

"The trouble is cookbooks don't get specific enough," Marian said. "When they say to beat an egg, wouldn't you assume that means to roll it around on the counter and smack it a few times? Then directions will say things like, *Add prepared horseradish,* but they never explain what *prepared* means."

There was a slight wistfulness to her humor, suggesting a desire to keep trying.

After dinner, Marian found Dan and Dora. "Nobody told me marriage would be such hard work," she said.

Dora laughed. "Why on earth would we have told you? After all, we wanted you in the family," she said warmly.

Marian sighed. "I'm so afraid of being a disappointment to Leaf. How am I going to make this work?"

Dora knew the secret. "Just love him, Marian," she said.

"Oh, I do! It's just that when we got married, I was so sure I was at the end of my troubles."

Dan honked his nose cheerfully. "You were," he said, winking at Dora. "You just didn't know which end."

It felt good to laugh with them. Marian loved having a family.

What If It's Too Late?

As soon as the dinner dishes were clean and back in the cupboard, Marian said, "Come sit on the porch with me, Hetty. I need to talk to you a minute." They linked arms and sat down close to one another.

"What in the world am I, Hetty?" Marian sighed. "I'm not sure if I'm your mother or your friend. And what am I to Leaf? I haven't learned to be a wife yet. Or even how to cook. And I felt so stupid asking you to sew up your father's trousers, after I'd offered to do it."

Marian took a deep breath. "Then there's my brother Joseph," she said. "He's so much like my stepfather Joey that I liked him right away. I'm glad Joey always talked about me and wanted Joseph to come looking for me. But," she added, "I don't even know how to be a sister to him!"

"It does seem like an awful lot to figure out all at once," Hetty said. "Things didn't exactly come at you one at a time! It's kind of like when I first started at Haxton Academy. Everything there seemed so overwhelming, I was afraid to open my mouth to talk. Because of that feeling, even the things I would have been good at kind of froze up.

"It got a lot better after my headmistress helped me. It was an absolute miracle! Aunt Freydis asked me what I was most interested in learning, then she worked with me on the list I gave her.

"And it always helped that I could tell everything to Papa. I usually went in the forest and talked to Hannah when Papa couldn't be there."

Marian was listening for more.

"When you and Father used to go for long walks," said Hetty, "was he quizzing you about whether you would be making apple strudel for him every other Sunday and how good you were at darning socks?"

"No, it wasn't at all like that," Marian laughed. "You know how Leaf loves biographies and nature books. We both do. We had too many other ideas to bother discussing strudel!"

"Here's what I think, Marian: you're just what we all want you to be, and you just don't know it! You've never made any promises to be anything else. Besides," Hetty continued, "getting all worried about doing the typical-wife-and-mother stuff is just going to make the very best part of you freeze up. Nobody wants the part of you we like most of all to stop working."

Marian's eyes brightened. She thought, *Reading is what I do best. Maybe I'm not such a dud after all; I'm a really good librarian. My mother did have a point. If you can read, you can cook. Or do just about anything. It can open up the world! Like Hetty says, I just need to unfreeze.*

"Actually," whispered Hetty, "maybe we need you for a friend, most of all,"

We? wondered Marian. She remained silent a moment then her words came gently. "You and I were friends before we ever met, Hetty. Dora and I spent a lot of time choosing books for you. The things you liked to read told me a lot about you."

Hetty lowered her eyes.

"What is it, Hetty?"

"Oh, Marian . . . I've made such a mess of things. I feel awful about not telling anyone. I'm so miserable, and I can't even talk to you about it. At least you didn't make a promise like I did," said Hetty. "One you couldn't believe in."

Hetty's lip trembled. "The trouble is I believe in keeping promises," she said. "Whatever they are."

"Did I hear you say, 'Whatever they are?'" asked Marian. She didn't wait for a response, but gripped Hetty's hand. "Sometimes there are promises that shouldn't be made in the first place. If it was a bad idea, I hope there's a fair way to unmake it."

A tear rolled down Hetty's cheek. "But what if it's too late?" said Hetty. "Maybe it's so messed up that there's nothing good to do about it. Except to keep the promise for its own sake."

Saying Goodbye to Morgan

Morgan would be getting married tomorrow. Hetty ran her fingers along a crack in Hannah's bark and closed her eyes. She hoped when she opened them again she would discover it was all just a bad dream.

Maybe some warm summer night, Morgan and I will be sitting on our squeaky porch swing watching the fireflies and he'll say, "Do you remember when you dreamed I was marrying someone else?" Then we'll both laugh so hard we cry. After we've gained control of ourselves, he'll say how absolutely unthinkable that would be!

Then he would apologize. He'd say that didn't mean he'd consider me some sort of nut if I thought that way. So, of course I would remind him I had fallen out of the tree once!

We would go on like that until we could hardly breathe for all the laughing.

Hetty opened her eyes. Still she saw nothing but the wretched truth staring back at her. Tomorrow Morgan would indeed vanish from her foolish dreams.

When she squeezed her eyes shut, a tear dampened Hannah's smooth bark. She vowed to stop pretending.

It's hard to imagine I'll never see him again. Surely he must feel how desperate I am to say one small goodbye. I hurt all over with the wanting of it.

If only I could look at him one last time. Even from a distance he would know how much I love him for being such a dear friend.

I know he'll come. He'll come because I want him to so much.

Hetty sought the comfort of Hannah's smooth branch and listened for Morgan.

There was a magical rustling of leaves some distance below. Hetty couldn't make herself look, for fear of being mistaken. The air became still, as it appeared to await some statement of its meaning. Even Hannah seemed to be holding her breath. Hetty could hear a suggestion of hesitant motion beneath her.

It was Morgan. He looked up through the leaves and found Hetty there just as he had wished her to be. A soft breeze floated her silken hair around her face. Her eyes opened. She looked at him as if there was no one else in the world.

Hetty felt her heart pounding in her throat.

"I love you, Morgan," she said. "I wish it was me marrying you, instead. I've loved you since I was twelve years old."

She looked down into the deep sadness of his blue eyes. She could see the little flecks of brown, but only in her memory.

"Can't I marry you, Morgan?"

He met her question with quiet. It was a sickening quietness.

Morgan looked down at his hands as if wishing them to do something. They hung helplessly at the ends of his arms, where they had always been. Yet they felt separate from his body and no longer seemed to belong there. Morgan knew they did not; they were meant to be reaching for Hetty. He looked up to where she lay clinging to the limb.

Hetty thought of her family, and the charade she had used to successfully hide her sadness from them. Between sobs she whispered, "I can't bear the pretending anymore."

The situation was so impossible! She began to cry softly.

"It's too late, Hetty," said Morgan. His voice was hollow.

He had become accustomed to the hollow and empty sound of his voice. He knew it made a loud and clear announcement. It seemed to say *Hey, everybody, Morgan Morganthal can't conceal his broken heart!*

Rather absently, he noticed an ant was feeling its way up a crack in Hannah's trunk. He saw the insect climb quickly and with determination, letting nothing stop its progress, no matter how difficult.

Morgan watched the tiny creature conquer the bumps and depressions. The corners of his eyes crinkled with intensity. His mind focused on what Hetty's father had told him: *Decide on what you want. And if it's right, pay the price.*

Morgan looked up through the lacy leaves toward Hetty. Her pale cheeks were brightened somewhat by the little pink splotches that had come with her tears. The sun, shining through the softness of her hair, played silvery games against the clouds above her.

So fragile was the scene that Morgan felt afraid even to breathe. He felt all joy and sorrow came together in that one moment, so intense was the turmoil in his thoughts.

I'll have so much to work out. We'll need to turn our entire world upside down. Both of us.

There's my father, Hetty's parents and her father, Leaf. There's Katrinka and Phil. What a monstrous thing to do to Katrinka.

We'll have to start sending wedding presents back, too. I mustn't think right now about the party tents that are all over our property. How do we tell the hundreds of guests we're canceling the wedding?

He looked around in desperation, as if somewhere in this forest there might be an answer to the mess he was about to cause.

He remembered a row of dominoes he had helped Melinda set up around her bedroom, across the hallway and into his room. Before they were all in place, she had bumped one by accident. In no time, they all knocked each other down. It took forever getting them picked up and in the proper boxes.

Morgan smiled up at Hetty. A blush of color came over her as she met his gaze.

"We have a few details to take care of first, Hetty," he said. "But tell me what you have in mind."

"Now!" cried Hetty. "Why not now, Morgan?"

Hetty blinked with surprise at her own words. She knew how unrealistic it was to have such dreams at the age of seventeen. Her time could not be now, and maybe Morgan was getting ready to tell her so.

He did not.

It was only by gripping onto Hannah that she could control the trembling of her hands.

A soft breeze lifted his whispered words to calm her. "You could never know what this means to me," he said.

Looking up at her with wonder and amazement, Morgan considered the whole situation. He felt cleansed by the relief that washed over him, in spite of the embarrassing complications ahead.

Golden flecks of light seemed to gather from nowhere. They swirled magically around Hetty, brightening her cheeks and eyelashes. The glow formed a halo in the softness of her hair, and Morgan felt a thrill of reverence at the sight of her.

Soon he was by her side, answering her need for reassurance. He wanted nothing more than to comfort her for a very long time. To hold her forever, blending his thoughts and feelings with hers.

He cupped her face with his hands and kissed away a tear.

Her lips were soft and pink and seemed to require something, and Morgan knew just what it was. He decided if one kiss was good, certainly two would be better. This proved to be true.

Hetty's eyes were full of love and joy. She had been saving her kiss just for him, with no hope that he would ever come for it. Now she rejoiced at the many hopes and dreams it awakened. Morgan could feel her relief and happiness while she trembled in his arms.

Though he longed to remain with her, Morgan knew he must go. His mind raced with a multitude of thoughts.

In order to cancel the many wedding plans, he would need to act quickly. He would need to hold several important conversations immediately.

Morgan smiled broadly. "I'll be back soon," he said. "We can talk then. But first I need to get Blossom's permission."

Hetty realized it would be feeding time for the animals, and Morgan could count on meeting Max there.

"Meanwhile," he said, "it'll give you a chance to think, too."

Reluctantly, Morgan left Hetty alone in Hannah. As he hurried away along the forest path, Hetty thrilled to hear his exultant, full-throated laugh.

It would take Morgan about an hour, but that would allow a little time for Hetty to plan what should come next. She watched the bright spots of sunlight filtering through the leaves and smiled to think of his return. She would climb high in Hannah so she could watch his dark hair shining in the sunlight as he came closer.

Morgan will probably need to give Blossom a quick shower with the hose after he feeds her and talks to Max.

I can use the time to plan how we should break the news to Mother and Papa. We'll need to explain it to Father and Marian and . . . everyone.

Suddenly, she felt the weight of her past secrecy lifting. It was replaced by the assurance of love she knew would come from her family, even if they weren't likely to fully understand. She thought about it as she waited.

The sky began to darken.

Morgan still hadn't returned by the time Hannah had grown cold. Hetty told herself Morgan would still come no matter how late it was.

Hours passed. She curled up against the trunk and tucked her skirt tightly around her legs for protection against the mosquitoes.

Leaf came to find her with a flashlight. Mother and Papa must have called him in alarm when they saw her bed was untouched.

"Marian has been worrying about you too, Hetty," he said. She heard the concern in his voice. She decided not to say anything until she had talked to Morgan.

Oh, Morgan! Did I just imagine you were going to come back for me? Was I supposed to understand it was just a joke?

Have I made a fool of myself?

CHAPTER EIGHT

The Something or Other of Her Dreams

Hetty removed her boots and flung herself onto the bed. Dora offered her some warm milk and buttered toast, but Hetty needed to be alone to think. She said she just wanted to sleep.

Next morning the glare of the sun awakened her, jarring her headache. She tried to stuff the plaid chintz curtains behind the edges of the blind. That didn't work, and the light still jabbed into her room in bright slashes.

Hetty resolved not to think about it.

What do I do now? Last night I was still thinking I'd need to talk it over with Morgan. Now I know he's no longer part of this. He'll be married in about an hour and all the pink stuff will happen to him.

In spite of being absolutely smothered in pink, he'll be smiling bravely at a long line of people. He'll remember everyone's name and ask about their children and their dogs. Nobody will want to move ahead in the reception line, as long as they can feel his firm handshake and have him look at them with his friendly smile and his deep blue eyes.

He'll say, "Mr. and Mrs. Johnson, we feel honored to have you here. May I introduce you to my wife? Oh, Katrinka, darling, would you mind terribly removing the mudpack that is opening your facial pores or whatever it does, to say hello to the Johnsons?

"I apologize, but unfortunately she is currently occupied with putting little pink curlers in her hair. I hope you will excuse her brief tardiness, because the reception started only ten minutes ago. She tries to give her full attention to detail. Please notice how carefully she has pushed back the cuticles of her dainty fingers.

"Mind you don't chip your nail polish, my beauty! Save your lovely hands for throwing your pink bouquet at your pink bridesmaids.

"What's the matter, Katrinka? You say your diamond isn't as big as the one King Nebucanoodle III gave the queen? I should be ashamed of myself!

Actually, I had planned to surprise you with a little something to take along on our all-pink honeymoon. I shall bestow it upon you this instant, if you will please cut into the pink cake."

She'll cut into the cake. Concealed in it she will find a pink four-door Cadillac with mink-trimmed seats. When she snaps her fingers, the servants will efficiently remove a mammoth quantity of icing.

Inside, she will find an enormous something-or-other sparkling on the dashboard. Is it a trophy? No, upon closer inspection, it turns out to be the diamond ring of her dreams!

Due to its weight, it cannot be lifted from its position against the windshield; however, she is able to greet the remaining guests with her left hand in the ring and her right extended across the pearl-encrusted bodice of her wedding dress and out the window of her new car.

Suddenly Hetty didn't feel very good about herself; she knew something was not right in her heart. In the past, she had successfully consoled herself with her thinking. Now she found having unkind thoughts of Katrinka made her feel worse. She had to work things out in her mind.

She's not some sort of cartoon character. Katrinka and Morgan are both flesh and blood human beings, and they want to be happy like everyone else.

How would Morgan feel if he knew about my attitude? He'll be doing everything he can to start out right. He needs his friends to think positively, too.

I know I should think more kindly of Katrinka. And if she makes Morgan happy, I'll even try to like her.

Tra la la, Kaboom!

Hetty turned her face to the wall to avoid the irritating light. As she rolled over, a faint echo chattered from the springs of the mattress.

Maybe the fringe on the blanket would give her fingers something to do.

Twist and smooth; twist and smooth.

*I hope you will excuse her brief tardiness, because
the reception started only ten minutes ago.*

Whatever she tried to do, still the wedding occupied her mind. It remained like a pink monster sticking out its tongue at her.

She tried to think of something that could help at such a time.

Marian once said, "For heaven's sake, Hetty! Don't forget your parents used to be your age once. Just because you can't remember being older, it doesn't mean they can't remember being young. Give them a try. They probably didn't think their folks would understand either."

But that isn't how I feel at all. After this day is over, I'll be able to talk to them, and they'll understand.

Maybe they already have a sense of what I said to Morgan, and they could be waiting for me to approach them about it.

When Father went into the forest to find me, I wonder if he could tell the birds knew something, or if maybe the trees seemed somehow different to him. It's as if Leaf knows how the forest and all the woodland creatures think. Was there something the woods could tell him about me? It's easy to imagine.

People can give off a scent, with fear and other emotions. Could that have happened when I spoke the way I did to Morgan? Maybe the scent of my feelings is forever preserved in the wood, along with my tears. Or in Hannah's rings. . . .

Father can read about the life of a tree that way. Maybe he would read it and see that it's the pitiful story of a girl who didn't know any better.

A hundred years from now, maybe a woodsman will cut Hannah down and learn about it by reading her rings.

Hetty's sorrow extended to the loss of Hannah. It was almost unbearable to think that someone would cut her down. She felt apologetic toward Hannah for giving it even a passing thought.

She cast around for other ideas to occupy her time. "I mustn't act like a victim," She thought. "I'm responsible for what I said. If I weren't, it would be like admitting to myself I'm powerless."

Hetty remembered a talk she once had with Dora. They had been on the back patio. The weather was clear and sunny, and there was a steady ocean breeze smelling of salt and sea life.

It was the kind of day I like inventing in my imagination. Especially when I know Morgan's going soaring.

I thought Mother would be happy with the whole world like I was, so it seemed like the time to bring up something I'd been wondering about.

I asked, "When you had the baby that died, how long did it take for you to get over it?"

Mother said, "I doubt that I ever will, completely. It just got easier to live with over time."

She told me that when I came along, it took a lot of energy just to keep me alive until after my heart operation. Between that and teaching me at home, there wasn't much time to indulge in moping around.

I asked how she would have recovered if I hadn't come so soon. Mother said she would have buried herself in books at first, and then found other ways to keep busy.

Maybe Leaf won't ever completely get over Anne's death. Maybe I'll never get over losing Morgan, but everyone has to keep on going somehow.

This time next year I'll be going to orientation at the university. It's good Morgan will have left by then to start law school, because I wouldn't want to meet him in the halls.

I can imagine how it would be. He'd say, "Fancy meeting you here! I'm so sorry I never got back with you at the tree. But as you know, Hetty, I never actually promised I would. I ran into a friend and we got talking about politics. I lost all track of time, till suddenly I realized the minister would be waiting."

I'll say, "Oh, that's fine, Morgan. It didn't inconvenience me at all. The fabric store was still open after you left me, so I was able to buy two and a half yards of black crepe to make myself a proper mourning dress. You see I consider myself a widow, now that you are no longer in my life.

"In fact, Morgan, it is I who must apologize to you. I should have found an alternate way to honor your memory. I couldn't throw myself on your funeral pyre, since there wasn't one.

"This is somewhat awkward for me to find that your remains are here walking around to be bumped into in the halls."

The hands of the clock were not moving fast enough. Hetty stood by the bed and stared at it until the minute hand lurched forward.

I can't stand what he must think of me. There he was, innocently going along . . . tra, la, la . . . making nice wedding plans, and suddenly, Kaboom! The day before the wedding, here I come, like a silly, star-struck teenager. I'm draped over the branch of a tree, and when I see him, I say, "Oh, by the way, why not pick me instead? We can play make believe. You be the daddy and I'll be the mommy. I'm too young, but who cares? We can have a little tea party up in Hannah and pretend it's the rest of the world that's out of step."

What will it be like without Morgan cheering for me? He says he loves to see me do things that make a difference.

Last month he actually came to the radio station when I read my essay. I couldn't believe it when I looked out into the audience and saw him sitting there with Father!

He says if I don't get a full scholarship it will mean the English department has taken leave of their senses.

"Morgan," she said aloud, "you can keep making good things happen. That's what you've always said to me. And you can be happy. I know you can!"

Hetty knew what had just come from her mouth was
utter nonsense. Not even her skillful imagination could cope with it.

A sick feeling came over her. Returning to her bed, she got in and pulled the covers up to shield her eyes.

An Excellent Plan

Hetty could picture Mother and Papa at the wedding reception.

Papa will be thanking Morgan for helping me become more comfortable with boys.

He'll say, "Thank you, Morgan. Hetty must have enjoyed working with the animals very much. In spite of all the extra hours she's worked, Hetty has come home radiantly happy every evening."

Mother will say, "We knew we could trust you with Hetty for the summer. Leaf felt that way too."

Morgan will say, "I'm afraid I have to apologize. I know you wanted her to become comfortable in my presence, but . . . "

Then Papa says to him, "You mustn't apologize! It worked, didn't it?"

Morgan will answer, "Oh, yes. Still . . . I'm so sorry, Dan. So very sorry." And he'll say, "It was wrong of me to have enjoyed such interesting conversations with her or to have respected her as an intelligent human being.

"It was unforgivable that I allowed her to feel like she was melting like butter whenever I so much as looked at her sideways," Morgan will say, "and I shall never forgive myself for allowing her to feel like she wanted to be with me the rest of her mortal life and beyond."

Morgan will go on like that saying, "I had no idea she had such grownup ideas. Like you, I thought she was just a child."

"Well she is, technically, Morgan," Papa will say.

"Yes," Morgan will answer, "and I feel entirely to blame for her speaking to me the naïve and foolish way she did. I didn't see it coming. I realize she has not confided in you."

Then to reassure him Morgan will say, "I'm sure there's nothing she has kept from you but her tender thoughts and emotions."

Papa will reply, "I know you're right."

Then he'll ask Morgan, "What would you do about Hetty now, if you were in my shoes? Do you have any advice for me?"

"Well, Dan, I would do as you've planned," Morgan will say. "When she goes to college next year, she can meet other boys. That way she can choose wisely."

Then maybe Morgan will make an observation. "Katrinka has known a lot of boys," he'll say. "Tall ones, short ones, blond ones, and redheads, and. . . . "

Morgan will decide to give up counting. Mostly because he doesn't want to add up Katrinka's former boyfriends on his fingers and toes there at the wedding. Morgan will probably shake his head and say only, "Well, you get the general idea."

At that point Morgan will reconsider what he thinks Papa should do about me. He'll say, "No, Dan. Actually, I think I would suggest encouraging Hetty to continue her education and develop her musical skills. She'll know what interests and ideas she should explore."

Suddenly, Morgan's face will light up with his final suggestion. "Maybe in about four years," he'll say, "when she feels ready to be a wife and mother, she should hurry back and marry me!"

Papa will answer, "Excellent plan, Morgan!" And Mother will clap her hands.

Then Morgan will say, "Oh, wait! I forgot I'm taken. Otherwise that would have been my suggestion."

Papa will say, "What a shame. And all because Hetty has been meddling with other people's lives, instead of her own."

Morgan will shake his head, and the blue of his eyes will become deeper and more serious. "I admire the way Hetty makes things happen," Morgan will say, "but she has kept a bad promise, and it made the wrong thing happen. That's why we're in this hopeless situation now."

The phone rang in the kitchen. Dora answered it as quietly as she could, to prevent disturbing Hetty. It was Leaf calling to learn if Hetty had improved.

"I'm not sure," she said. "I couldn't interest her in any breakfast this morning. It's unusual for her not to talk to us, or to you and Marian.

"When we got word about Morgan's accident, Dan and I decided not to tell her. If nothing else, Hetty would be disappointed to hear the wedding was cancelled.

"The maid who answered at the Morganthals' didn't know anything, except that it's critical. The family and Katrinka are at the hospital. She says they're mostly concerned about his internal injuries."

The Accident

Morgan's body lay still on the hospital bed, his face a sallow gray. Bustling nurses and men in white coats came and went. They appeared to be checking his vital signs with urgency.

The family hovered near the door, hoping to learn anything of his condition, yet they seldom saw more than the tangle of wires and tubes that cluttered the bilious green room.

Melinda said, "I don't think Mom could take this." Max nodded in agreement and watched his daughter pace up and down the hall.

Max and Melinda had arrived at the hospital the night before, and Phil followed close behind the ambulance to join them in the lobby.

"Katrinka should be here any minute," said Phil. He thought of how disturbing all this must be to his daughter.

Morgan was unconscious when Katrinka arrived, and Phil was proud of her for the way she braved the ordeal.

The local newspaper had requested an interview with her. Katrinka was willing to answer questions of the men who crowded around her with cameras, and she even put on her wedding dress and veil at the appointed time. This heightened their sympathy for the heartbroken, picture-perfect bride.

The wedding would have been newsworthy enough as the social highlight of the season, but its cancellation and the reasons for it were even more dramatic.

Phil and Max sat quietly on two stiff chairs in the corner of the large lobby. They had gone all night without a restful sleep, and were sobered by Morgan's puzzling condition.

Max stared straight ahead, his eyes glazed. He thought about the moments leading up to the accident.

Late in the afternoon, Morgan had come running from the direction of the forest, and was out of breath. He entered Blossom's pen and said, "Dad, we need to talk."

Max said, "If we're going to talk, I'll be in charge of what we talk about." There was a firm set to his chin. He moved a shovel from where Blossom might trample it, and continued.

"This business of our working together—it hasn't been too bad," said Max.

"It sometimes galls me, all you do for Melinda. But now I'm not sure why it should. I see how you have friends. Like Hetty . . ."

Morgan tried to break in at this point, but Max held up his hand to prevent the interruption. "And your friendship with Phil," he continued. "It doesn't make me mad like it used to."

"But Dad," Morgan said, interrupting as peaceably as possible. "There are so many things I try to do because of you," he said. "Frankly, your example is to blame. The way you are with the animals. And I admire your doing what's fair, even when it's hard. I'm glad for it. As your son, I want to follow your example."

Morgan pushed against Blossom's right rear leg to get her to move off the hose; then he continued. "I've seen how good you are to Phil. For years, you've made sure he had employment."

Max squinted at the sun. His words became heated. "I'm not as good as I seem. I take Phil's advice because he's smart." Max scowled and went on. "And he can help run the business."

"Why won't you let me admire you, Dad?" inquired Morgan, with an almost desperate sincerity.

"Come on, Morgan! You don't admire me. You just wish you did."

Morgan suddenly knew something about himself; he realized all these years his plans to marry Katrinka had been to please his father! He must say so now or forever lose his opportunity.

It was time to state his intentions. He must speak of Hetty.

Morgan said with determination, "Dad, I'm marrying the right girl. No matter how long it takes. . . . "

Both men were distracted by their emotions when Blossom slapped Morgan with her trunk, and in the same instant shifted her weight.

Max yelled a warning then helplessly watched as his son lost his balance.

With a horrific crunching of bones and flesh, the elephant trampled Morgan's body, mangling him under her massive feet.

CHAPTER NINE

In the Lobby

Max watched absently as a hospital volunteer prepared the lunch trays. The aroma of pot roast mingled with the smell of disinfectant. It disgusted him. The meals would go to the patients who were well enough to eat. Would Morgan ever eat again?

On the couch down the hall, he watched as Phil sat next to Melinda and reached for her hand to reassure her.

Max stood alone looking through the window, his face blank. His uneasy mind wandered for a time.

I've gone so long without feeling any emotions. At least I've attempted to. The man at Alcoholics Anonymous says it's sometimes that way for him too, but he's not giving up. His wife won't come to the meetings, either.

For some reason, I can be open and honest in those meetings, but it's hard to do it with my son.

Before the accident, why didn't Morgan come straight out and criticize me? The things he said were harder to bear than if he had.

If he pulls out of this, I'll never strike him again. Why do our tempers flare when we're together? I've hoped for his respect, but most of all I've wanted to deserve it.

If only my last conversation with Morgan had resolved our differences. I hate seeing the gap between what Morgan imagines me to be and what I really am. The difference is too great.

He would have been disappointed to learn the truth about what I've done to Phil. Now he may never hear it. As soon as Phil learns what I've done, I'll lose him as a friend. But I need to get it off my conscience.

As if on cue, Phil got down from the couch and slowly approached Max. Melinda resumed her pacing in the hall. Max suggested they sit someplace where their conversation would not be overheard. He knew Phil's neck ached when he stood looking up at tall people.

Max looked toward his son's door and said, "If Morgan gains consciousness, the chaplain can perform the wedding here just as easily. I have the papers all ready," he added. "Katrinka will never want for anything."

"Max, don't go through with your inheritance plan," said Phil. "Truthfully, I wasn't sure you meant it. Please don't feel any obligation to go through with it now."

Max frowned and stroked his chin. He looked at his friend and said, "I gave my word. I need you to accept the arrangement for my sake."

Phil did not respond. Max watched Morgan's door open, but the nurse who hurried away avoided his gaze.

He tightened his fist as he tried to work things out in his mind.

The presence of Hetty Lawrence over the summer has had a profound effect on Morgan and me. The three of us were like comfortable friends when she was there. She had a way of softening my feelings toward Morgan. I believe it worked the other way as well.

I'm not so sure about Morgan's friendship with Katrinka. I've been wondering if there's something lacking in that relationship. But I guess Morgan's last words should erase my doubts. He said Katrinka was the right girl, so I'll have to comply with his wishes.

Phil spoke next. "There's no reason to do it, Max," he said. "You've been generous enough toward me. And there's another concern," he continued. "I don't want Katrinka wondering if money is the reason Morgan chose her."

"You can assure Katrinka money is not his motivation," said Max. "Morgan has no idea about this plan of mine."

Max clenched his jaw and looked at the wall. He knew there would be no relief for his conscience until telling Phil.

He said, "But there's something I have to make up to you. I did something inexcusable.

"When your big chance came," said Max, "I simply couldn't let you go. The biggest circus in the world wanted you, but all I could think of was myself."

Max looked at the floor. "I lied about your character in my letter to them. When I put it in the mail I hated myself, yet I never retracted my words.

"I needed you then like I need you now," said Max. "You would have been set for life, if you'd gotten that job. But after all our years working together, I couldn't see how I could go on if you left. I simply don't know how I would have done it."

Phil appeared stunned. He and his wife had been amazed that he was wanted for such an exciting and responsible job. There was to be so much opportunity for making policy decisions, and they would have allowed him to continue working as a clown as long as he wanted. He always puzzled over why the offer had dried up.

Phil looked at his friend. Max looked worn and broken.

There was no logical response that came into his mind, but Phil raised his hand and placed it on Max's shoulder. In the simple gesture Max recognized a pledge of continued friendship and forgiveness. He could only hope time would confirm that.

Max was overcome with shame for what he had done, yet his burden of guilt felt lighter for his having revealed it.

Later that night, whispers were heard at the nurses' station. "You should have seen the dwarf and the dark-haired guy," they said. "They were laughing and juggling oranges and bananas in the lobby."

The Green Cheese Moon

The guests must be leaving the reception by now, thought Hetty. *It's over.* Breathing deeply, she forced her shoulders back.

She had not yet forgiven the morning sun for its intrusion. Maybe the afternoon sun would make her feel better if she allowed it to. She opened the blinds and tucked back the curtains.

Hetty went through all her usual preparations for facing the day, but everything felt somehow useless, or colorless and unreal. Her face looked the same in the mirror, so maybe nobody would know it felt like she wasn't in there anymore.

A new thought occurred to her.

If I pretend that nothing about Morgan ever happened to me, and try to keep it all to myself, I may recover better. By letting it fester, or allowing myself to mourn, it could ruin my whole life. If I whine publicly, it would only embarrass Morgan.

Hetty opened her bedroom door a crack. She heard quiet voices in the kitchen. It was as she had hoped. Leaf had come and was downstairs talking to Papa.

She found herself on the stairs going toward the soft voices she loved to hear.

"Father?"

"Yes," Leaf replied, "and I brought Marian. We've come to see how you're feeling."

"Thank you, I'm doing fine." She looked around to see the relief on their faces. Papa put an arm around her shoulders to give her a squeeze. "You had us worried, Hetty."

"I'm sorry, Papa. I thought I'd wait till the wedding was over."

"There was no need for that, Hetty," said Dora. "The wedding had to be postponed. Now that you're doing better, you'll probably want to offer your comfort to Melinda."

"Comfort? What's the matter?" Hetty looked around at their faces.

"Don't worry," said Dora, "The wedding is still going to be performed by the hospital chaplain. When Morgan gains consciousness, that is. We know you've been close to Melinda, so we thought you'd want to know."

"I have to go see him! I need to be there!" cried Hetty.

"Melinda will appreciate that," said Papa.

Dan was pleased at Hetty's concern for her friend, as he drove her to the hospital, but he was surprised she was so frantic about the delays in traffic. He let her out at the hospital entrance so she could run straight in.

There was a blur of hopelessness in the green surroundings of the lobby. Hetty didn't wait for the elevator, but ran up the long stairway instead.

Morgan's door was at the top of the stairs directly in front of her. It had a commanding sign in bold letters that stated, *No Visitors Allowed*. The name *Morganthal* was written in grease pencil to the right.

From the nearby desk, a nurse guarded the door like a troll. She scowled at Hetty with surly suspicion.

Max stood alone against the window. His silhouette was very like Morgan's. His face, though often lacking expression, was now lined with grief. Hetty's arms went around him.

In her embrace, Max recognized her emotions went far beyond mere sympathy for him. He held her tight and they rocked gently for a moment.

It was a gesture of comfort he had been wanting to give someone, sometime. It had been in there waiting for a need to come along. Max had little practice in providing comfort. Melinda had never needed him.

"The others are in the cafeteria," he said. "I'm glad you've come, even if you can't see Morgan. It means a lot to me."

"Papa told me Blossom did it," she said.

Max nodded. "Maybe it was my yelling that startled her. I blame myself," he added. "Maybe it reminded Blossom of the trainer who abused her." Max stared out the window.

"When it happened," he said, "Morgan had just told me Katrinka was the right girl. That was the last thing. . . ."

It felt to Hetty as if the air was being sucked out of her. *No,* she thought, *It's just a mistake! She's not the right girl. Max could say the moon is made of green cheese, but that doesn't make it true.* She searched her mind. There had to be some way to clear up this awful misunderstanding.

The elevator door to the right of them opened. Katrinka scurried through the opening and rushed past Max and Hetty. She wore her long veil, but had removed her wedding dress. It now hung behind the nurses' station, where she could slip into it quickly, should the time come.

Max turned to Hetty. "We decided Katrinka could go in," he said. "The doctor thought it might be the best medicine of all. But I'm not so sure."

The Visitor

Katrinka arranged her hair gracefully against the lines of her tiara. She spread the lace veil to frame her face to best advantage, and approached the desk. Drawing back her lips to reveal her pearly teeth, she whispered a request in her most demure voice.

Enchanted, the nurse opened Morgan's door, and ushered Katrinka to Morgan's side so she could be alone with him.

Next to Morgan's bed, Katrinka sat in a stiff chair and rearranged her veil. She frowned. It simply would not cooperate. *Oh, well. He can't see me anyway,* she sighed.

When she finally forced herself to look at Morgan, she was dissatisfied to see his slack jaw, the pale grayish skin, and limp hands.

She had envisioned a handsome groom of solid dignity standing next to her. This one had a bedraggled look. Morgan would be unable to flash his white smile to dazzle the guests and make all the other girls jealous of her. Somebody ought to give him a shave.

The sight of him triggered a startling thought. There might not be a wedding at all!

Everything was going wrong. The pink and white striped canopies had been removed from the Morganthal estate last night. All the pink flowers had wilted in the sun, and the little pink cakes had melted.

The pictures of her in the paper were not as pretty as she had hoped, either. The photographer who posed her by the door had taken a particularly unflattering picture. The latch behind her looked like an extension of her nose. Her cousin Libby said she looked like Jimmy Durante.

No matter. She knew how to make the best of her situation. She must always remember how her daddy handled things like this. He had taught her how to live with the things you can't change. She looked away from the grim sight stretched out on the bed, and thought.

Daddy, how can I be strong and keep smiling? You are my inspiration. I know you love me.

I wish you'd never sent me away to school. Every day I looked for a letter from you and I cried myself to sleep at night.

Morgan is always polite, and you say he'll be good to me. I don't mind so much that he doesn't love me, as long as you do. Maybe he will learn to.

I know you want him for a son. I can do this for you. Especially if I think about the money.

Morgan moaned and tugged at the tube in his nose.

Katrinka was frightened. "Better not do that, Honeybun!" she said.

He was still again, and Katrinka wondered if she should leave quickly before he did something she couldn't control. If he tossed himself over the bed rails, maybe she'd get the blame for it.

It seemed as if he was straining to say something. He had not responded to anyone yet, so she knew it was not likely.

Katrinka felt uneasy as his restless breathing became more rapid.

"Don't try to talk, Morgan," she said. "You might mess up your wires and things."

There was a furrow between his dark eyebrows. The attempted exertion appeared to tire him. Finally Katrinka heard Morgan speak softly.

As if in prayer, he whispered, "Hetty . . . Hetty . . . ," then lay exhausted.

"No, no, Morgan! It's your Katrinka! It's Trink, Honeybun." Her eyes filled with tears. Her hand shook as she wiped her cheeks.

Breathing deeply to gain control of her voice, she replied with courage born of determination.

"Hetty is out with Joseph again," she said, forcing a little laugh. "You know how kids are at that age!"

Loopy

The Lawrence kitchen was still glowing with the afternoon sun.

Dora smiled at Leaf and Marian. "Well, I guess Hetty's fine," she said, "but I always enjoy an excuse for you to come over."

Leaf had an idea. "We could get together at the cottage later. Why don't you come over after Dan and Hetty get back from the hospital," he said. "We have some slides of our wedding. When you see them, it will be obvious to you that Gorilla's parents were the photographers." Leaf chuckled. "Gorilla's in most of them."

"She was the perfect flower girl," said Dora. She was amused to learn Gordon and Camilla had invented the name *Gorilla* by combining their two names.

Marian listened quietly as the others laughed and enjoyed the conversation; however, she could think of nothing but Hetty. She remembered a recent conversation when Hetty had said, "I believe in keeping promises, no matter what they are." Her tears had revealed the rest of the story.

"Hetty's not fine," Marian burst out. "She's not all right. I'm sure of it."

She looked at the three surprised faces. "Am I the only one who sees it? I say she's positively loopy over Morgan Morganthal."

Leaf was stunned. "But he's marrying someone else," he said, "and she's just a child."

"Is she, Leaf?" The three listeners paused to consider the significance of that question.

Marian continued to amaze Leaf. She had voiced such a bold opinion. He looked at her with combined shock and admiration.

"Hetty did seem shaken when I found her last night," said Leaf. "But truthfully, I don't find the idea at all likely, Marian."

Marian wasn't through. "Hetty appears strangely anxious to get Morgan and Katrinka married," she said. "Haven't you wondered why? I think it's her panicky attempt to stop caring about Morgan," she said. "She's gone so far overboard, it's unnatural. I believe it's all baloney."

Dora was reminded of the lines from *Hamlet:* "The lady doth protest too much, methinks." She wondered if those words of Shakespeare might apply to Hetty.

"She's never been one to have foolish crushes," she said, "but if you're right, Marian, I only hope it won't be too devastating for her."

This Is Home

Hetty curled up in a chair in the dark corner of the lobby. Papa had left her with some nickels, expecting her to reach him by payphone when she wanted to go home.

This is home, she thought, *because Morgan is here.*

She stared at his door and listened to the quiet voices of Phil Wallace and Max down the hall. She contemplated Morgan's future.

I wish I could see ahead to the possibility of his living out his dreams.

He should be in the library of his own law office. I can just see him searching through his law books for just the right case—the way his hair falls down over his forehead—then he'll jump up and clap his hands! He does that when he discovers something.

If only Morgan will live! They mustn't let him die. I can accept anything but that. He's so full of ideas and possibilities.

Hetty remembered Morgan's account of a long walk he once took out of a burn area. He'd been dropped at the fire by a Ford tri-motor, the plane affectionately known as *The Tin Goose.* Morgan stopped to ask an old farmer for directions back to the ranger station. The man said, "Go through the meadow two sees, then turn right and go one more see. You can't miss it."

Morgan asked him what he meant by that. The answer was that you walk to the farthest landmark you can see. When you get to it, you go once again as far as you can see, and so on. Just keep focused on one spot at a time, till you're there.

Hetty continued to watch the door. *I must see that Morgan lives. That will be my first see. His recovery will be enough to start with. That should be my focus,* she thought.

After that, I'll look for something else to hope for in his future.

He likes having children around him. He should have one on his shoulders and another holding his hand. They could watch the birds fly over the ocean till they disappear into the clouds.

Morgan wants to see Max as a grandfather. He imagines him doing magic tricks and teaching the children to juggle.

The soaring competition will have to wait. He'll miss the one in England this year. If only he could attend the one two years from now. It's hard to see that far ahead for him. I need to envision one step at a time. But how do we get to that point?

Morgan tells me about a man at the Edgemont Senior Community Center who became a good friend. Morgan sat with him when he was dying. The man couldn't talk at all, but Morgan saw recognition in his eyes. He was sure he understood kindness and heard whatever Morgan said. It made his death easier for both of them.

I could do that for Morgan, if he needs me.

I hope somehow he can tell I'm near him. Suppose he doesn't know I care and never finds out I've come!

If only I could sing to Morgan, to him alone, and no one else.

I want to be very close, where he will know my thoughts are just of him, where we can breathe the same air. Where my breath will mingle with his, to give strength to his lungs. Maybe my wanting to make his body strong will make it happen. I believe all things are possible.

Hetty closed her eyes and played with her memories.

At the party she had given for Morgan and Katrinka, Max had taken five photographs. The entire time he was taking the pictures, Morgan kept his arm around Hetty's waist. In the past, she had tried to bury that memory, but it always resisted her half-hearted efforts.

Hetty now allowed herself to imagine both Morgan's arms around her. She could even imagine his breath on her cheek. She blushed, and the slightest smile formed on her lips.

Morgan's door opened, and Katrinka came out. She didn't notice anyone was there at first. Then Hetty coughed to make her presence known. She rose quickly from her chair and asked, "Is there any change? Do you know any more?"

"Oh, it's you," said Katrinka. "He's real bad. They say he can't have any visitors. Right now, any excitement could take his life, you know. His condition's real fragile, so nobody can go in there. Except me." She smoothed her veil.

"Max says we can be married the minute he wakes up. He's arranged it with the chaplain. Other than that, thanks for asking. I'll tell him you wanted to know."

She bustled to the elevator. Katrinka had to go home for a nap.

CHAPTER TEN

Something Is Better Than Nothing

Dr. Davidson was speaking to Max and Melinda in the lobby. Phil stood with them, but Hetty stayed a tactful distance away and listened attentively.

"I understand your concern," said the doctor. "It's only been two days since the accident. It always seems longer for the family. The reason you're not getting a clear prognosis from anyone on the medical staff is that frankly, they're puzzled," he said. "Morgan should be doing better than he is. His vital signs should be improving, yet his condition is still serious.

"It didn't even seem to help when his fiancée came to visit him. Morgan appears to have given up. I've seen how fragile life can be when the patient doesn't have the will to live."

Melinda noticed Hetty and hurried to where she was standing.

"I was sure you'd come!" she cried. "You knew I'd need you. I don't know what I would have done without Phil, but now—Oh, Hetty, I'm so glad you're here."

Melinda could no longer veil her emotions and sobbed openly. Hetty led her to the couch. She placed her sweater around Melinda's shoulders and handed her a tissue.

"It's good you and Max have each other," Hetty said. "I'm sure you're a great comfort to your father."

Melinda looked at Hetty curiously. "I don't know about that," she said, blowing her nose.

Hetty thought of how Morgan longed to improve the bonds within his family. She reported a conversation she remembered. "Your dad told Morgan he's pleased about you . . . the way you've turned out," said Hetty.

"Really?" Melinda brightened somewhat with surprise.

"Yes," Hetty continued. "I know he was wishing you had been free this summer. Max thought it would have been fun working together."

Melinda sniffed. "Maybe I should . . . talk to him? About Morgan, I mean. I'm not sure what to say."

"Anything at all, I suppose," said Hetty. She thought of all the things she could say about Morgan.

Melinda continued. "Dad will think it's strange, after never talking before."

Hetty looked toward Morgan's door. The nurse glowered. The scowl on her face had become more ominous with practice.

Hetty longed for any glimpse of Morgan. "Anything is better than nothing at all, Melinda," she said.

Lying Down on the Job

Hetty had dozed off that evening at about ten o'clock. The hospital lobby had been quiet at the time, except for the rustle of papers and the swish of skirts as the night nurses came and went. She was only vaguely aware of her surroundings.

Someone now covered her gently. It was Phil laying his jacket across her.

"She gave her sweater to Melinda," he whispered to someone.

All was quiet once more.

After five minutes or so, there was another voice. It was Max Morganthal speaking quietly for only Phil to hear.

"It seems like between the two of us, we've accomplished an impressive number of wrong moves," he said.

"You could say we've had a problem or two," Phil replied. "Both of us lost family time, but we can still make it up."

There was more stillness. It was interrupted as a woman called for the nurse. The rustle of a starched dress was heard briefly then died down.

"It still tempts me when I see other people with alcohol," Max whispered, "and it scares me," he added.

"Then don't look at them, Max." Phil shifted his weight and chose to be silent for some time.

It began to rain, gently at first, then in heavy drops that splashed from the deep windowsills onto the panes of glass.

"I mean it, Max. Don't look where you don't want to go. It seems like every tightrope walker has to learn that some time or another. It scares them half to death to look down. If they want to get to the other side safely then that's where they ought to look."

The voices were pleasant. They drew Hetty into a welcome drowsiness.

She listened to the steady rain and hoped it would cleanse the outside world.

Maybe tomorrow will be fresh and new, and Morgan will jump up, clap his hands, and say, "Let's go, girls! Time to prune the bushes at school," Or, "Hop in the car. We can't be late for banding the birds," or, "If we hurry, you can see the Navy blimp."

Phil shifted his weight again. He was uncomfortable with the height of his chair. "What is it about you tall people?" he said, "You must like to watch us dwarfs dangle our feet."

"Don't flatter yourself," laughed Max. "It takes more than that to amuse your audience."

Phil hummed a tune briefly then asked, "Remember when we did our rubber Volkswagen act?"

"You think I could forget? You were the most ridiculous hood ornament that's ever been shot from a cannon!" Max grinned.

"That was about as good as it gets," Phil agreed. "If you weren't so good-looking, we'd still be at it."

"Oh, don't be such a clown!"

"Well, it's true. You merely walk into the bleachers and she falls head over heels for you."

"You think it was easy powdering her date's nose with a bathmat?" asked Max. "Besides, look where it got me. She doesn't approve of my being a clown. She never did."

"Now, wait just a doggone minute, Max. What were you when she married you?"

There was a long silence while Max seemed to mull that over.

"I can hear you thinking, Max," said Phil.

"Right. I can hear you being short, Phil," said Max.

"While we're on the subject," said Phil, "I've always wanted my daughter to marry a man who can hold his head higher than mine. No offense, my friend, but since his run-in with Blossom, your boy's been kind of lying down on the job."

There was a pause. "Whatever happens to Morgan," said Max, "you're welcome to stay on at the gatehouse. You can always call it home."

He looked at Morgan's door. "Katrinka too," he added. "If it comes to that."

The Confident Woman

At the stroke of midnight, Dan entered the hospital. He folded his umbrella and saw Phil preparing to leave by the same door.

After learning from Phil that the doctors had nothing new to report, Dan thought it appropriate to tell him of Morgan's high praise.

"Morgan has appreciated a lifetime of guidance from you," Dan said.

"Thanks for saying so," said Phil. "I know how helpful your legal advice has been to him. I haven't seen him much this summer, myself."

"I'm aware of that," said Dan. "In fact Morgan expressed his concern just this week. He hopes you're not offended."

"Morgan could never offend me," said Phil. "He's like a son."

The two of them paused to watch the rain splash in the parking lot.

Phil thought of how relieved he was that Morgan would indeed become his son. That would be the best outcome for everyone.

With time, Morgan would learn to love Katrinka. *She'll mature,* he thought. *I don't need to keep protesting the marriage or the inheritance. Max usually gets what he wants, and he wants this wedding. I've said enough to have a clear conscience when they go ahead with it.*

Dan nodded good night to Phil. "Well, I'm here to pick up Hetty," he said.

"She's alone up there," said Phil. "Asleep on the couch. I'd be surprised if she wants to leave."

"Maybe you're right," said Dan. "She didn't ask me to come. Her mother wanted me to bring her something to eat, anyway."

Phil went out into the rain with no jacket, and Dan went up the elevator with no idea what to expect. He found Hetty in control of her emotions. "Can you just sit with me, Papa?" she asked.

Dan gave Hetty the tuna fish sandwich. She gave him an appreciative hug after which he honked his nose.

Their years of understanding one another would continue. Dan knew the meaning of her words: she felt gratitude for his company; however, that was all she wanted. Dan looked at her with a new appreciation.

What has made Hetty into the confident woman she is? She seems calm. Yet such a transformation doesn't happen without a struggle. It's as if she understands her place within some bigger plan. Is it because she knows who she is and where she's going?

Marian was right. It's all about Morgan. We always knew she would look to someone else; every parent knows it will happen. We just didn't expect it so soon.

Even though Hetty doesn't want to discuss it now, we'll need to be available when her heart's broken.

Remorse

Early next morning, Hetty found herself alone in the lobby. When she looked at Morgan's door, she saw no evidence of change.

It was after six o'clock, but the low clouds hid any sign that the sun intended to rise. After a more reasonable hour, she would call her home so the family wouldn't worry. Rain still dribbled down the windowpanes. She felt grateful for the warmth and comfort of Phil's coat.

Hetty straightened the magazines on the end table. They felt limp from sopping up the humidity in the air. It would be difficult to keep from going limp herself.

I can't let myself feel like a victim, she thought, *or I'll be of no use to anyone. I have to think clearly.*

From the window, the world seemed no cleaner. The puddles in the parking lot below were iridescent with oil. Hetty noticed the figure of a girl running across the grass toward the hospital. It must be an emergency. She looked somewhat like Katrinka, but strings of rain-soaked hair streamed down her face. The wet skirt clinging to her legs slowed her running.

Hetty sat down to pull up her socks and tighten her bootlaces. There wasn't much else she could do, but she could think. She remembered something Morgan had learned: the way to develop backbone is to do something hard every day. She resolved to do whatever hard thing was required of her today.

Her thoughts were interrupted when the elevator stopped before her. It opened to reveal a droopy spectacle, still soaked with rain. It was the girl she had seen running toward the entrance of the hospital.

Approaching Hetty, the girl appeared anxious to speak to her; however, only a gasping sound came from her throat. Her nose was running, and she sobbed incoherently.

Once in control of her panting, she began. "I'm sorry I didn't tell you," she cried. "I should've. But I didn't mean any harm. I only lied to him because . . . well, I wondered if it might even be true. About Joseph, I mean. It could've been." She sobbed more convulsively.

Puzzled, Hetty asked uncertainly, "Katrinka?"

Katrinka continued her disjointed explanation. "Maybe Morgan said your . . . you know. . . . Maybe he knew what he was saying," she sobbed. "He must hate me . . . when I didn't come get you." The words tumbled out with confusion.

"Oh, please don't tell Daddy!" she cried.

Mascara ran down her cheeks. Her lipstick was smeared across her mouth, yet Katrinka seemed unconcerned with her appearance.

Whether she was shivering with the cold or shuddering with remorse, her guilt-driven gestures made her seem suddenly childlike.

When Hetty took both her hands and looked directly at her, Katrinka averted her eyes. The lashes on her left eye had become unglued and hung by the corner. They were entirely missing from the right side.

"First let's get you dry," suggested Hetty. She led her to the ladies' room.

After blotting a great deal of water from Katrinka's hair and clothing, Hetty took Phil's jacket from her own shoulders to place around the unhappy girl. The two of them returned to the lobby.

"What if he dies and I go to hell!" wailed Katrinka.

Hetty waited patiently in case Katrinka might surprise her further. Then it happened. Katrinka faltered, her lips trembled, and she whispered the words Hetty would never forget.

"It's you he wants, Hetty . . . it's you."

With that, Katrinka turned and hurried down the stairs.

Hetty stood still to reflect on the moment.

Her mind exaggerated the beauty of every sensation. The slapping of Katrinka's shoes in the stairwell sounded intensely musical; where Katrinka had stood, a puddle of water made the light it reflected into a dazzling celebration.

As Hetty's eyes explored Morgan's door, it seemed larger and more significant than ever. Her whole body tingled with eagerness to enter, but she knew to restrain her excitement. She would wait for the door to be left unguarded.

Only the Angels

Morgan felt powerless and trapped. He was pinned under a monster of his own making. His mouth could not form words, nor could his muscles escape the dark heaviness that immobilized them. While he lay still, his thoughts labored to overcome the confines of his damaged body.

The words that whirled through Morgan's nightmares caused pain far beyond that of any physical damage he had endured.

Hetty won't be coming. She's with Joseph. Has she invited him to Hannah? No, that's unthinkable! It's her special place. Surely, she won't grant him that privilege.

But maybe he'll give her an empty candy wrapper. Then she'll smile at him, and when he winks back at her. . . . Oh, please, Hetty! Don't accept a candy wrapper from Joseph!

Dad won't be coming, either. He said it's unfortunate I'm his son.

But that was long ago, and we can be friends now.

I should have been talking to Melinda all along. She's always needed me, but I should have seen how I need her, too. She'll be my sister forever; surely Melinda will come!

Katrinka has been to see me.

Only Hetty knows my thoughts, and she won't be coming.

At last Morgan's door was left unguarded and slightly ajar. Hetty entered. She saw Morgan's chest rise and fall, and she rejoiced at the sweetness of being in his presence. Quietly she approached with reverence for life itself. Yet it felt to her as if the mere memory of an imperfect dream or an unkind thought could end the frail miracle of his quiet breathing.

There has to be a way to reach you, Morgan. How can I let you know I have come? How do I tell you my thoughts?

I will find a way or make one.

Max and Phil arrived and stood in the hall. Each had approached the small opening in the door, but upon seeing

Hetty there, thought it best to step away. Hetty could hear their muffled voices outside the door.

The nurse continued to police the area like a troll. It ran counter to the advice and judgment of the hospital personnel to allow visitors into the room. If she should discover Hetty's violation, there would be an unpleasant confrontation. She had been looking without success for that girl with the untamed hair and the clunky boots.

Upon peering through the crack in the door, she scowled. Hetty was in there. At last she had discovered the little nuisance, and it would be a pleasure to expel her with dispatch.

Max and Phil glanced at one another, and with one accord they barred the door against the nurse. They gave her firm instructions. She must allow Hetty to remain there undisturbed.

Hetty marveled at Morgan's forehead, so white and pure. As if some master sculptor had seen the beauty of his soul. Maybe he was created out of someone's dreams on a day filled with light; dreams of possibilities and all things perfect.

Morgan's dark eyebrows were at rest. His eyes were closed, yet Hetty imagined they would once again open to reveal the blue depth of their gentleness.

A dense stubble was beginning to darken his chin. What a treasured new discovery it was! She would keep it stored in her memory along with some of the stories he told and ideas he shared.

Suddenly Morgan was still.

As Hetty drew closer, fear clutched her. A scream caught in her throat, but was silenced by a flicker of optimism.

Was his heart beating? She laid her head on his chest and listened until a steady pulsating heartbeat relieved her fears.

Tears of gratitude filled her eyes and flowed onto the white sheets that covered Morgan's chest.

She clung there in silence for fear words might disturb the fragile balance between what was real and what was hoped for.

Morgan felt a soothing warmth on his chest. The sweet fragrance of honeysuckle reached his nostrils . . . or was it the scent of Hetty. . . .

Weightless as swan's down, the pale wisps of her hair formed a silken halo . . . swirling in his head together with flecks of dancing sunlight. He wanted to spread his wings and fly above the world.

If I could fly with her through the clouds, beyond the sky and higher, where everything is clean and bright—brighter and brighter until the perfect day. . . .

I want to reach for the light I see around her.

Hetty's cheeks warmed his chest. Each breath she took was shared with him; they were dancers whose beating hearts were music enough. The dark heaviness that imprisoned him lifted with the sun's warmth.

The hint of a smile began to form at the corners of his mouth. Perhaps the whispered words of some dream were trying to come from his lips.

A surge of power, and Morgan felt strength in his hands. Only the angels could hear his tender thoughts, as his fingers reached for the softness of her hair.

Then out of the quietness came the words of his dream. "My Hetty. . . . " he said. "My girl. . . . "

P.S. EXCERPTS FROM CORRESPONDENCE

August 25, 1955

My dearest Hetty,

The joy of knowing what awaits us . . . and our decision to wait four years . . . the two are in constant conflict! I can hardly speak your name for the thrill it gives me. . . .

    Yours,

        Morgan

September 6, 1955

Dear College Girl!

I still can't believe it! You and Morgan! I'm so glad you're going to be my sister-in-law.

The whole class is kind of in shock. I think they get the connection between Morgan canceling his wedding and you leaving school early. Anyway, Mrs. Fairburn talked to the class about it, and she was wonderful.

It's great she could arrange early enrollment for you. My senior year won't be as fun without you, though.

I can tell my parents liked the letter you sent them. I've seen Dad carrying it around with him.

    Love,

        Melinda

September 20, 1955

Dearest Morgan,

. . . I know you are right. If we speak freely of our feelings, it will be even more difficult to stick with our four-year plan. I'll try to control my pen. But only if you promise to remember there is love in every ordinary word I write. . . . I can't remember a time when I didn't love you. . . .

Your Hetty

October 1, 1955

Dear Blossom,

I've written a short poem for you:

When Trampling On Organs,
Why Morgan's?

I know you share in the hope that Morgan will feel better and mend fast. I'm so glad he can be up in a wheelchair now. If you show this rhyme to him, please do so from a respectful distance. With kindest personal regards from your forgiving friend,

Hetty Lawrence

P.S. Do not kiss him for me. I hope to do it myself.

October 20, 1955

Hetty's journal entry sent to Morgan:

I thought of Morgan all day, and how I'll be seeing him in only nine weeks. I think I spend as much time wishing I could write him as I would in doing so. . . . I've about worn out his letters, reading them. . . . The condition of his body has absolutely no bearing on whether I want to marry him. I'm not sure he believes me. He's afraid I don't know what I'm saying, but I do. I guess I'll need to do the proposing again, if he is to believe me.

November 7, 1955

Dear Melinda,

Thanks for your letter.

Morgan called me! With only one payphone in the dorm, we couldn't talk long. We decided not to count it as one of our monthly letters! I asked him if he went to his Halloween party as Vargo the Magnificent, and there was the longest silence! He seemed embarrassed that I figured out he was Vargo. He explained how your father and Phil needed him to catch the trainer in the act of using the barbed whip. He said they couldn't let their plan leak. I assured him you hadn't told me, but he already knew he could count on you. . . .

Love,

Hetty

March 28, 1956

Dear Hetty,

Happy eighteenth birthday. . . . I hope this doesn't count as a letter just because I wasn't willing to pass over such an important landmark day. . . . As hard as it is to be apart, I would find it even harder to be together and keep to our plans. . . . I'm trying to learn patience. . . .

Your Morgan

If only I could tell you my thoughts.

May 27, 1956

Dear Morgan,

I'm trying not to tell you how much I love you, like we decided. . . . I appreciate how the family's taking us seriously. . . . I can't believe you would actually try starting law school in September! You amaze me. . . . If only I could tell you all my thoughts! They're very mushy, so please read my mind. . . .

     Love,

       Hetty

January 12, 1957

Dear Morgan,

The classmate I told you about (the one who's singing in the quartet with me) has given me some great ideas for breathing exercises to improve my voice. . . .

I know it's against the rules we decided on, but couldn't I say I love you every once in a while?

       Hetty

February 30, 1957

Dear Hetty,

I sense the excitement about your singing. Tell me more! Your classmate must be a good singer. I'm counting the days until I see you. I really think it's best that we stick with the rules we decided on, so I'm not going to weaken my resolve by telling you how very much I love you and want to be with you.

       Morgan

May 15, 1957

Dear Morgan,

I'm glad your leg is so much better. With Mother's polio and Papa's Forest Service accident, our family already does enough limping. Still, not everyone can boast of being squashed by an elephant. . . . I told my classmate about you, and he wondered if you knew his best friend who's there in law school too. . . . He's a year younger than you.

I must remember to ask his name. . . . All my dreams are of you.

My love, Hetty

May 18, 1957

Dear Hetty,

You make me insane! I thought your classmate was a girl . . . . I'm trying hard not to think about it. . . .

Love,

Morgan

May 19, 1957

Morgan's journal entry sent to Hetty:

When I told Hetty I thought she should meet other boys, what was I thinking! It was all talk. It was to help her be sure of her decision, but my heart wasn't in it. I need to stop worrying and concentrate on my studies.

May 23, 1957

Dear Morgan,

I saw no reason to tell you Ken wanted to marry me, and I'm sorry his friend mentioned it. It just seemed like a nice friendship, so I didn't see it coming. He has one major flaw. He's not you. I've only been going along with your suggestion that I get to know other boys because you wanted me to. Can I stop now? Why should I spend time with anyone else? It's you I want.

    Hetty

August 18, 1958

Dear Hetty,

Remind me why I signed up for smoke-jumping this summer. Do you want to know what I think of our plans? And being apart for four years? I think it is stupid! I wish we were working in the same forest. Next time I jump out of the plane, I'll wave toward your lookout, even if we can't see each other.

    Love,
      Morgan

December 6, 1958

Dearest Morgan,

. . . You know my answer. It's always been yes. . . . I can hardly breathe, I'm so happy. . . .

    I love you,
      Hetty

December 12, 1958

My own Hetty,

.... I'm sorry you've been concerned about a Christmas gift for me. Your answer was all I wanted. ... When I think of our future and remember our past, it makes every day seem indescribably bright and beautiful. ...

Your Morgan

December 18, 1958

Dear Marian and Father,

Morgan and I can hardly wait to see you and tell you our plans! Can we celebrate Christmas all together at the cottage? Your letter meant a lot to me, Marian. I love having you and Father together. Thank you for giving me so much credit for it!

Love,

Hetty

December 18, 1958

Dear Mother and Papa,

I can hardly believe this will be my last Christmas before I become Hetty Morganthal. .... I have loved the name Lawrence because it came from you, the dearest parents ever ....

I love you,

Hetty

Don't be too sure we've seen the last of Katrinka. And what is the effect of Tilly Teller's gossip column? Will the animal abuser take his revenge? Can Morgan and Hetty overcome the challenges that threaten their future together?

Find the answers in third-in-series, *Hetty or Not*.

ABOUT THE AUTHOR

Martha Sears West grew up daydreaming and climbing trees in Bethesda, Maryland. She received her B.A. degree in linguistics from the University of Maryland. Now the mother of three and grandmother of ten, West hopes everyone with children can see teenagers as the joy and inspiration she found hers to be.

Hetty is the first novel in the Hetty Series by Martha Sears West. She has also written and illustrated *Hetty Happens; Hetty or Not; Honeymoon Summer; Hetty on Hold; It's Me, Pippa!; Love Me on Purpose; Deliriously Yours.*

Longer than Forevermore; Rhymes and Doodles from a Wind-up Toy; and *Jake, Dad, and the Worm; Jacques and the Forbidden Christmas.*

COLOPHON

The Bembo Typeface

Bembo is a classic typeface that displays the characteristics that identify Old Style, humanist designs. It was drawn by Aldus Manutius and first used in 1496 for a 60-page text about a journey to Mount Aetna by a young humanist poet, Pietro Bembo, later a cardinal and secretary to Pope Leo X.

More recently, Bembo is the typeface used for volumes in the Everyman's Library series. Monotype Bembo is generally regarded as one of the most handsome revivals of Manutius' 15th century roman type.

The font size of the italic sections in Hetty is 13; otherwise, font size 12.5 has been used in the body of the text.